T0041525

Also by the author:

Brimingham, 35 Miles
Snakesin Road

This Ditch-Walking Love

James Braziel

Livingston Press
The University of West Alabama

ISBN 13: trade paper 978-1-60489-278-9
ISBN 13: hardcover 978-1-60489-279-6
ISBN 13: e-book 978-1-60489-280-2

Library of Congress Control Number 2021930404
Printed on acid-free paper
Printed in the United States of America by
Publishers Graphics

Hardcover binding by: HF Group
Typesetting and page layout: Joe Taylor

Proofreading: Aubrey Elmore
Brooke Barger, Claire Banberg

Cover Photo: Richard Bickel

www.richardbickelphotography.com

Thanks to the following places where these storesi first appeared.

Appalachian Heritage —— "Watersmeet"

Berkley Fiction Review —— "Wanting a Lover Man"

Fiction Southeast —— "Baby Forever"

The Literary Review —— "The Boobie Trap"

Map Literary —— "Jick's Chevrolet"

Map Literary —— "Vittate"

Newfound —— "Asleep in Peggy's Grace"

100 Word Story —— "Where the Stars Fall Together"

Phantom Drift Limited —— "Ferris Wheel"

Porter Fleming Literary Competition —— *"Tulipwood"*

Potato Eyes —— "Hawk"

Raleigh Review —— "Last Time Bo Played the Blues"

RE:AL —— "Jack Who Loves to Paint"

Zone 3 —— "Shiner"

I owe the completion of these stories to a grant from The Alabama State Council on the Arts and to my three readers—Ada, Tina, and Jim—and my editor, Joe.

Livingston Press is part of The University of West Alabama,
and thereby has non-profit status.
Donations are tax-deductible.

6 5 4 3 2 1

Contents

This Ditch-Walking Love

For Tina

Saplings

1.

Watersmeet

—

There's a ridge I need to climb ever since Toadman died.

He loved toads. Got his nickname that way, hanging out with them and brushing the splotches on their backs like the splotches were grey pools of lily pad hair. Toadman and I biked and walked to every creek in the county, for we are not a county of rivers—just rills and rivulets that widen into creeks. I followed Toadman cause he knew where the frogs hid in summer on the cool north banks beneath mud funks and old pine logs that had tumbled down. He found a copperhead like that once. Got bit straight through his wading thumb.

See, Toadman always put his wading thumb in thc water first cause the other frogs thought it was a fellow frog. He never wanted them to be afraid. Copperhead thought he'd come upon a fellow frog, too. One moment, Toadman was combing the water quiet, next he was hollering louder than the coyotes beyond Zeller Hoyt's place at four in the morning when I can't sleep and wish I could. Toadman's hand zipped up, and the snake wiggled off. It splashed down a beautiful pipe-copper rain. I unplugged my boots from the shallows to help, but the fangs had torn through the front and come out back busting Toadman's nail off its bed. Every time I pressed the nail down, it popped up. Blood oozed out. His thumb throbbed.

"You my best friend," Toadman said. First time he'd ever said it like he better speak what was on his mind quick, his face swirling in a pink fuzzy sweat.

I told him straight out, "You ain't dying, Brother." He was not my real brother but a brother in that other way, truer to claim when no blood between you. We was kids then, and I meant what I said, and he meant what he said as if certain words when spoken right can become real. Ain't so, I promise.

"When I die, do me one favor," Toadman said.

"You ain't going to die," I said.

"Cut my thumb off, Beal." Beal is my name. "Put it in at The Cross, so it grows into a frog." He shoved his thumb in my face.

"You are talking crazy," I said. I mean, Toadman was already a magical thinker, but cutting off his thumb? A thumb turning into a frog? A thumb pretending to be a frog was one thing, but—

"Promise," he yelled.

People get delusional. I knew this even then, especially with the sun burning hot like it was. I said, "All right now. All right," to calm him. "Listen, you ain't dying," though I was none too sure. He had turned white like all the blood had gone out of him, and his arteries were sucking the poison in deep.

We scaled the top of Hanna Ridge, zigzagged it fast, and shuffled down the other side to Bull's Holler, which we had walked to from our homes hours ago.

"Shouldn't you put a turnip on my arm?" He stepped in close to me, ready, but I couldn't figure out what he meant by turnip-on-my-arm.

"You know," he said louder after my longish silence, "to keep the poison in my thumb."

"Tourniquet," I said.

"Oh, yeah, *that*," Toadman said and began to count the broken yellow lines on the highway. Nothing worse than feeling you're not smart enough. Before he said "Oh," I thought maybe he did mean turnip, some witchy thing like his wading thumb, like his brushing the invisible hairs on the big fat lily toads, which made them bend their legs into his hand. They appreciated what he did, how he held them.

My real brother, Junius, volunteered for Snead Fire and Rescue. He had put a tourniquet on an injured man once.

"I think you got a dry bite," I said to Toadman. This came from another one of Junius' stories of saving others. Truth is, I didn't know if Toadman had a dry bite or not. I just wanted him to relax. I said, "I'll put a tourniquet on you just to be safe," and pulled off my shirt and sweat-drenched it round his arm above his elbow.

He was still breathing hard from our up-and-over Hanna. Both of us had fallen at several junctures on brown needles and leaves wet from yesterday's rain, and I could feel his blood pump quick under the cloth where I made the knot.

He nodded at me, thankful, and I at him like best friends and brothers do. Then we walked up Bull's Holler, caught a ride to the hospital, a fellow out of Allgood I didn't know. And Toadman was perfectly okay.

"You have no venom. Not a drop."

"Are you sure?" he asked the doctor more than once.

"None." The doctor smiled. "You've been lucky today,

young man. A dry bite." The doctor wore a long milky coat. All the walls and nurses and equipment and lights gave off the same unyielding milkiness. Toadman's parents hadn't shown up yet when we were told this. No one could locate them. But even without the reassurances of parents, we were relieved.

I inhaled my first full breath since the copperhead waggled off Toadman's thumb, and I started on a hiccup jag that lasted well over an hour. Those walls were so white. It hurt to take it all in, as if we'd gone to the sun and peeled the orange back to the center and out spilled hot blinding seeds.

*

The ridge I need to climb is Osanippa. You have to come to it from Bull's Holler. Go up-and-over Hanna to Middle Mountain, which isn't much of a mountain—everything in our county has been carved out of the Cumberland Plateau. Middle takes you on to Osanippa. Follow its crest to a sheer rock drop. Below is the place we call The Cross, which is where all our creeks come together—Foot, Peggy Grace, Big, Pike, and Luna—to make the start of the Locust Fork River.

The waterways lay out like a compass you can see from atop Osanippa. For a long time, I wanted to take a girl up there. No one in particular, but I like brown hair, and for hips to sway like loose brown curls, and for her to want me coming in close without hesitation.

Between Peggy Grace and Foot, the water spits out a sand beach every spring. Most people come in that way to smooch or have a beer party. Some have perished jumping off Osanippa, slammed their heads into the rock slick bottom, and broke their necks just like that. My brother Junius said *just like that* with the snap of his fingers whenever telling stories of the drunk bodies he'd pulled out. Boon Chastain—"His lips got torn off by catfish." Chester Rounds—"No ears after we trawled him out of the rapids. Funeral parlor had to break his bones to set him in his casket right." And the one girl—"Maya Maya." My brother never gave anything away about her, but double names are rare and easy for me to remember. Whenever he spoke of Maya Maya, he shook his head and drew his breath in like he wanted her back.

Some people have jumped off Osanippa and lived. When the water's rushing high—this is key they say. If you're not too tall, this helps, too. Most important is to know how to float like a feather, not fall like a rock. Make the air hold you up, so by the time you're down cutting through the wet, you won't go far in fast. "Water," Tanya Preston, who supposedly made the jump and who isn't tall, explained to a group of us at Saterfield's oncc, "is just heavy air, ribbons of heavy air. Think of it," she said, "that way."

I've dreamed it that way—how my body might float through the fall, how a strong crosswind might lift my elbows and ankles. Once in the cool wet, my fat legs and arms would bubble me up to the surface quick, and I'd be okay. There was one dream I was a kingfisher, and I split the water easy. All from the tallest place in the county, where you can see this earth farther than from anywhere else.

*

After the hospital visit, for the rest of that summer, Toadman and I went to the north banks of creeks for frogs. He used his other thumb but without much success. Turns out, it wasn't born a frog. In August we started school and found other best friends, other brothers to be around.

I call those days The Before Time. Same as in the Bible. Only Junius is the marker in my story. The Before Time happened before he rushed into a trailer thinking someone was stuck inside. He shouldered the door down, and with just that little extra push of air, the fire caught huge and hot. He ran like a furious train, but it was his ashes, no one else's were found, when things cooled.

I have looked after my mother ever since. This is The After Time. Her thoughts stay tangled and cannot untangle. Most days, she digs her nails into her palms until they bleed, and she says Junius' name or my father's name. My father passed, not long after I was born. I didn't know him except he was called Fleet, and some mornings she says, "Good morning, Fleet," to me.

"I'm not him," I have to tell her. "Sorry I can't be your man today." Sometimes I do tell her yes to give her comfort. She pats my shoulders, but my bones and skin are all wrong. She knows I'm lying.

"Well, when Fleet gets here, he'll know what." Or she says, "I wish June would come for dinner," and trails off cause she can't place either man outside herself into the small length of room she wanders. By lunch she's doing the nervous digging, again. I can't pry her nails loose until she naps. I cup her hands, pour peroxide over the wounds. They froth a brown, scabby blood. She flinches but doesn't wake when I dab the puss-froth clean.

Lots of people have died I don't care about. Live long enough and you'll close yourself from others, too, I promise. I didn't care about my brother as much as I should've. There was a big difference in our ages, and he only let me into his world when he wanted, keeping back what it was of him I could have. But when Toadman passed, that was different. Maybe it was the way it happened, shot by his own father, or maybe it was because we had the one summer together catching frogs—which I enjoyed doing more than anything else I've done—or maybe it was cause I saved his life once, which turned out not to be enough, which turned out to be at the time a mere dry bite and not as big a deal. I'd made a promise to him though. And a promise to a dead brother is one you keep.

*

This is how it happened.

One afternoon I was riding around with Junius, the wind doing its howl, punching the doors of the truck as we squiggled down wet clay roads. I wasn't thirteen yet, but he'd started to let me drink just to get the taste, which I hated. But wanting to be a grown man, I kept sipping tiny on that rotten wood water. It was winter, and we drove around the county, looking at different places he hunted. Sometimes we parked to check on his stands. During the driving part, we inspected ditches for deer tracks. Once, we found panther tracks in a fan of clay. My brother always talked about some big buck, a sixteen-pointer he had hunted forever. Lived up on Nectar

Gourd, the part where no one had set down a concrete slab or staked a trailer home. Now there was a panther to hunt on the Gourd, too.

That afternoon my brother got a call from Sheriff Pinkie Sligh—his crazy name gets him half his votes, I swear. He was with state troopers and Alabama Power on County Road 27. A tractor-trailer had run off into a pole. Driver had nodded off and was dead. Electricity knocked out for miles. Pinkie wore many hats—he was also Chief of Snead Fire and Rescue—so he called Junius to help with another problem until he could get done.

"I'll take care of it," my brother said.

"Be careful," Pinkie said. "The man just walked off the mountain and left his kid up there. Tess Wyte found him going in circles in her yard. You know what he told her? Accident. He didn't mean to do it." I heard this much from my brother's phone and leaned closer to hear more.

My brother nodded. "The man's in shock, Pinkie," was all he said.

"Tess keeps calling me every minute to get him out of her yard. She won't let him in the house. Her daughter Oneida's with some new boy in Gatlinburg. No help at all, that girl. You know their place?"

"Near Double Run," my brother said and said goodbye. Then he said to me, "We've got something to do, Little." Little was my nickname cause, as he put it, I was little compared to him. And at the time this was true.

I straightened up and said, "What's going on?" I wanted to get rid of my beer before we got to this place of eventual sheriffs. But Junius kept pushing the gas so hard I was afraid to crack open the door and toss the can. My door might shoot open and pull me to the rock and dirt road. Always, I thought of the worst ways to die. Too cold to let the window down. So I drank the last swallows of wood piss quick. "Someone hurt?"

"You know the Lace boy? About your age," he said.

"Toadman?" I said.

"Toadman?" My brother's mouth acted like it had just eaten turned meat.

"Eckford," I said. "Eckford Lace."

"Yeah, him." My brother wiggled around to move his hands better on the wheel. If someone been coming round those dirt road corners, they been knocked back dead.

"Well, what's going on?"

*

I'm heading out, decision made, not driving. I'm walking to Bull's Holler like it should be done, and from there Osanippa. We've had lots of rain and one ice storm so far this winter, but today has been a February thawer. The sun is out good. Whatever cold the ground has held onto, it's having to give back to the air, which is glad to take it and sweep the cold far, far up to the sky for the sun to melt. A windy day with lots of crossing. I've got my knife—my brother's. In my left pocket, I have the thumb.

Not Toadman's. He died when I was almost thirteen and I'm twenty-two now. His thumb is all worm-eaten-ash. I've survived in The After Time without a brother for years. No, this thumb belongs to someone found on Zeller Hoyt's place a few days ago.

Let me back up—we've had a run of murders in the county, and we're not a county of murders. Or murderers, for that matter. But for the last year, about every two months, a body gets found off Highway 231, or behind someone's barn, or—and this was the strangest place yet—someone got wrapped up in one of Zeller Hoyt's barbed wire fences.

When the bodies appear, they're headless, footless, handless. No purse, no wallet. This is what Sheriff Pinkie Sligh has focused on. Someone is murdering people to take their identity and their cards, then leaving the authorities no way to figure out who the dead are—no hands, no feet, no teeth. And the killer, or killers, are dumping bodies in our part of Alabama cause we're in the middle of Jesus Christ nowhere. Probably drug smugglers out of the "Devil's playground of Florida"—that's Pinkie's theory. We haven't had a rash of missing persons in the county, so the folks we find are from somewhere else. This much we know.

At Zeller Hoyt's I found a hand—I'm a volunteer, took my brother's place once I got old enough—and the killer, or killers, had cut it loose and lost it. Must have spilled out of their satchel. Which is all that squares cause with the hand, the dead person could be identified. Only, I kept it.

People puke when they come upon these bodies. Maybe they recognize something of themselves torn up or they make onto the figures the figure of someone they love or have loved. My stomach never rattles. When I found the hand at the tree line, blood-sticky and palish, I thought . . . I don't know what I was thinking, really, but I wanted it, so I hushed it under pine needles and later came back, wiped those needles off. I've kept the hand outside in a Ziploc bag, which I know is crazy. I should've taken it to Sheriff Pinkie Sligh, and at this point, I've put myself in a situation cause he's going to wonder about me.

Yesterday as I turned the bruised fingers round, barely able to get them to flex through the plastic, I thought of my promise to Toadman. I know my actions are pure craziness, but earlier this morning, I did what had to be done. I sawed clean down the jointed bone, cut the thumb loose and washed it and burned the rest of the hand in a barrel-fire with the trash I burn every Saturday. Mother's up. She's been fed. I'm heading to Osanippa.

*

When Junius and I pulled up to Tess Wyte's house, Toadman's father was chicken walking in the large yard that touches the road, black seed bahia curling under the wind. He carried his shotgun in the sling of his arm. Tess was secured behind her window in a robe that pulled her wrinkles tight. She clutched a phone.

"You stay in the truck, Little," my brother said. He slammed his door shut. He walked around the hood Mr. Lace started to circle the opposite direction.

"I know this isn't good, but—" Junius paused for a beat, which he did whenever he switched his tack. "We need to go up and get your son. If you just—" But Toadman's father paid no attention.

"Come on, Mr. Lace," my brother said.

His voice sounded tiny from inside the closed off cab where I'd sunk down, my eyes just above the vinyl of the door, where the wind kept pounding. I was ready to duck into the sweet feed and spilled coffee and beer on the floor, where the warmth of the truck had dwindled with the heater off.

Then my brother, he walked up to Mr. Lace, took hold the barrel end of the shotgun. He stopped that man from walking.

"I'm taking this," Junius said. Broke the man's spell. You have to understand, my brother was big, train big, and when he took hold of things, he didn't let go until ready. I thought maybe Toadman's father would fight him. A fight he would lose, but when people get delusional, they do what they shouldn't.

"Why you here?" Mr. Lace said.

"To help," my brother said. He pointed to the house window. "Tess called Pinkie. He sent me and my brother." He pointed to the truck, then pointed to himself. "I'm Junius Chambers. My father was Fleet."

"Marvelle your mother?" Mr. Lace said.

"She is," my brother said.

"I remember when your father passed." Mr. Lace stared at the ground after saying this, which in our county is a sign of respect.

"So do I. Now let's go get your son."

But he didn't budge, and Tess moved away from her window view.

I should be out there. If Toadman's father saw me and recognized me as his son's friend, maybe that would help the situation, break the man's spell wide open. I took the door handle. "One more second, out you go, Little," I promised in a whisper. I was about to say it louder when Toadman's father nodded his wattle neck, saving me from my heroics. He let go his shotgun, and my brother came over to put it in the rear window rack.

"What happened to Toadman?" I said.

"Get out," he said. He took the revolver from behind his seat. A small .22 full of hollow points, which could, if called upon, bring damage to a body. My brother by his size and weight alone could bring damage, but he kept that .22 for practice on beer cans we finished off. He'd let me shoot it a few times, so I understood how. It had belonged to our father. It was milk-handled and silver.

He turned and pulled his shirt up, pushed the silver along his spine into his waistband. He closed the door quiet. I got out and closed mine. The wind poured around me, and Junius said to Mr. Lace, "You got to take us where your son is. Going to take all three of us to carry him down."

"I'm not sure exactly," Mr. Lace said. He was still out in the grass huffing like no way he'd ever get his breath right. Toadman had breathed the same way after the copperhead struck his thumb. Something in me wanted to shake that man until he said where Toadman was. Something else in my shoulders and legs started to fall back. My brother held me with his eyes then, his look a warning—*Don't fall apart on me, Little.*

"If you can get us close," my brother said. "Retrace as best you can."

He didn't respond, and my brother said, "We have to get Eckford now."

That's when the man stopped huffing. He paused like before and chicken nodded. It all happened when he heard the name Eckford. Funny how someone's name can stop you, whatever motion you're in. Suddenly that someone is in front of you, just behind your eyes, gesturing for you to come closer, even though they are not there at all.

Toadman's father looked at me then, yet it was like he never knew me. Maybe he couldn't remember—it had been over a year since I was in his house. Or maybe it was just the shock of what he'd done. I will tell you this, he wasn't someone I recognized any longer.

*

How my father died. Got a tattoo a friend done on him, which got infected. Worse than that, he got tetanus and his body swole until the swelling broke his bones. This is the story my brother gave. My mother will tell me nothing of it.

My brother got a tattoo once. Of a hawk, right on his arm, right where you could see. My mother got so angry at him, she kept saying, "What'd you do that for? Why you do that, June?" She kept her arms crossed, uncrossing them only to pick at stray curls on her head.

"Had to," he told her.

I got so angry, I punched him in the tattoo. Wanted to make that blue-green hawk fly.

My brother took my head. For a second I thought he had snapped me out of my socket. He told me, "Punch it, again, Little." He let me go.

So I thumped the hawk harder and harder like I could break through to the flesh, get inside the belly of the bird, the arm of my brother—they were one in the same—only then would I stop. And my brother, it had to hurt him some because the way his mouth turned, yet all he said once I stopped throwing punches, too tired to throw anymore, "See, Little, see. I'm alive. So very much alive."

*

We found the place where Toadman was on the ridge in a skirt of pines, and my brother took Toadman's shotgun off the brown straw, clicked the red shells out clean. He told me to put them in my pocket. I fumbled the shells but didn't drop them. I stuffed my pocket full. And Junius handed the gun over to me before I could whimper.

Flat on the ground, face up, was someone I'd called a brother. Only Toadman no longer looked scared like that summer afternoon after the copperhead. Death makes the difference. Death had carried away his fear.

My brother asked Mr. Lace what happened.

"Stock of my gun hit the ground." He pointed along the earth until, "There," he settled on a lightered stump. "Gun shot my boy in the back is what happened. Accident's what it was. We were just walking."

The tops of the pines bowed how the wind wanted. If they bowed down anymore, they might spring back with such a fury, the cold air would be flung into the sky and away from us, and we would be safe. But the cold kept sinking, the wind pushing.

My brother held Toadman's neck for a pulse, then lifted his body slightly at the shoulders, the ankles. Already it was like the body wasn't my friend, just a shell. His heart had stopped a while ago. Leaves and dirt had soaked up his blood. The dry bite's promise kept.

What did the bite on his thumb feel like now? Maybe those bumps of healed scar were still in place. Or maybe when he passed, all his old wounds opened again and bled. I had never known a dead body, not up close, so I made up a story about what death could do.

I was holding the shotgun like my brother wanted and could not lift Toadman's hand to see if I was right. My brother, he tapped the center of a hole he found on Toadman's chest, which is what my brother did whenever he found bullet wounds on the deer he killed.

"Came in that way," I said, and Junius looked up. He held the air between us to make it silent cause he understood things quicker than me.

"Let's take your son down," he said to Mr. Lace. "I'll take the arms, each of you one of the legs."

But Mr. Lace heard what I said. My first mistake. At least I think that's what happened. Or maybe it was my brother tapping near the hole in the chest. Or maybe Mr. Lace's lie couldn't hold him together any longer cause the man started running, scratching up leaves, to get to the top of the ridge. This one's name is Younger.

My brother dug a red shell out of my pocket, pulled the chamber open, clicked the shell in, and gave the shotgun back. All of this went so fast, the barrel was still warm from where I'd held it before, where I was holding it now. Time jumbled on itself. I didn't know what to do.

"You stay with Eckford," he said. "If you need this." He took the safety off.

I said nothing.

“You know how,” my brother said. “Just like the .22,” he said. I nodded. And he stepped into the trees, running.

*

So on this morning I climb. Up-and-over Hanna. Across the deer paths that mark Middle Mountain. There’s no more grey cloud to filter out. I am under the blue. The wind pushes me up and up until the crest of Osanippa is done, and I’m here. The highest point in the county. Straight down is The Cross where all our waters meet. First the rains. The rains funnel along rills and rivulets into wider and still wider pathways carrying off our iron dirt, our rocks, our dead branches. This place is where everything in the county eventually comes from one direction or another. This is where everything vanishes from us.

The water’s high today, swirling and clear to the pebbled bottom. In the center of The Cross, a smooth mossed rock juts out like a dog’s thirsty tongue reaching up from the earth to lap at the water.

The thumb I’m carrying is ready to become a frog if, just for a few seconds, I can have Toadman’s magical thinking. I’m ready. But there’s one last thing to tell.

*

“You know how,” my brother said. I nodded.

Sometimes you can make one mistake and get away with

it. Seldom two. I wasn't thinking quick like my brother, or maybe, no, the opposite, I thought too quick, wanting to compensate for being just twelve, for not knowing enough, and I set my finger at the trigger ready cause Mr. Lace, he'd be back—his legs running in reverse flickered on my brainpan. He'd come here, and I'd have to stop him from getting away with whatever he'd done, which, turned out, was shoot Toadman over a disagreement about fallen branches in their yard. This is what he confessed to Sheriff Pinkie Sligh later. Walking down the ridge, having not shot one quail, Mr. Lace said to his son, "I expect you to pick up every stick when we get home. Make the yard clean." Yesterday's storm had brought the branches down. But Toadman had two turtles in his room. He had a rabbit. And he wanted to see about them.

That summer when we were brothers, I came over to his house a good bit. His family kept the AC on. I shivered walking inside for my family had no AC money. Their living room smelled of sweet bacon grease and sugar tea, good smells, but his room carried the odor of soured wood, of old beer. The turtles in their aquarium and the rabbit in its cage didn't seem to mind, so I didn't.

"Where the frogs?" I asked. He never kept any frogs we found.

"If I brought one in, I'd have to let something here go," he said. "That's Lenore, Anna, and Essie." He pointed to the biggest turtle, a black shell crossed in yellow lines, then the smaller one, then the rabbit. He told me this on my first visit.

"But you could keep as many frogs as you want," I said.

"It'd get too crowded." He shrugged and I thought of the sour wood. My brother had said pets were thankless work. Toadman said, "Besides, I like letting the frogs go free. I can let Lenore, Anna, and Essie out for you, Beal, if you want."

"Just the rabbit," I said and he nodded. He popped open the cage door. He took Essie out and walked over, spilled her into my cupped palms. Black and white spotted, a little weighty and warm, the rabbit twitched as nervous as me, which made my blood begin to hum.

"You listening? You going to pick up those branches," was what Mr. Lace said as they walked down Younger Ridge. "We're not talking about this anymore. When we get home, you do what I say."

Toadman said something—he cussed his father. Or maybe he just said No. Whatever it was made his father turn, lift his shotgun and shoot Toadman, point blank, in the chest. Just like that. Point blank. And he loved his son. Loved his son very much.

And me, I was set on the trigger, ready for Mr. Lace, but off it went and shot my brother, just like that, as he turned.

I said what I couldn't hear—my eardrums had popped, the wind had hushed. I tried to hold the side where I hit him, put what had sagged out of him back in. My brother kept saying something in short breaths. He was on the ground, and the blood poured through my hands in the pulse of those breaths.

"Call Pinkie," his words spiraled into my ears until they took.

"I'm sorry," I said because my fingers kept sticking to the buttons on the phone. I mashed the wrong ones until I got through.

"I'm not good," my brother said. "Been shot. Little didn't mean—I'm the one gave him the gun, understand?" His tone shifted. “Get up here, Pinkie. Mr. Lace has run off. Follow the firebreak. We’re in a skirt of pines, halfway. Just get here.”

My brother said Sheriff Pinkie Sligh was on his way and to keep the phone close, and then he directed me on putting another shell in the shotgun’s chamber. “Watch for Mr. Lace,” he said. “Don’t be afraid,” he said. “Promise.”

I promised.

It wasn’t even the late part of the afternoon. The clouds had left and there was a lot of light. Still, I started to worry the dark would get here before they did. Nothing in the stories my brother told me helped me save him. But before he passed, I called, “You still there?” whenever he got quiet. I waited for a response.

“Over here, Little,” he said, like he used to tease when we played in our yard at night, and I couldn’t find him. *Tell me where you are, please*, I’d beg after running, then spinning, grabbing at the black and never him. I caught no moths, nothing, lost all my breath until, *I’m about to fall*, I’d warn. Gravity had put a dizzying ache in my head.

But before I hit the earth, he would loop his arms round my waist and pull me, hold me just off the ground and he would laugh—good god he laughed—shaking me and saying, *I got you, Little. I got you good.* The sudden stop brought a rush to my head, which brought light to my eyes the curl and color of lightning yellow. For a second, he had pushed the dark away, and I brushed my fingers over the dirt and grass and the round ends of his boots until he righted me.

“Over here, Little,” he said on Younger Ridge like he had said in the yard. Or he groaned or he murmured words I couldn’t put together into anything I knew. I netted my hands against the wound to make the best patch I could until my arms ached and fell. The blood turned cold and sticky in the wind. On my tongue, gunpowder, metal. I wanted water. The sun stayed on us, not moving it seemed.

"You still there?" I called, but time wasn't working right.

Mr. Lace had disappeared. If my brother had gone after him—my brother wasn't made for running up a ridge, I can tell you that. Like a train, he'd do good coming down. You wouldn't want to get in his way. But going up would've been much too hard, taken too much effort.

I thought of my father's milk-handled revolver, the hollow points, how they busted beer cans wide.

It wasn't until later when Sheriff Pinkie Sligh showed and took us down and the dogs cornered Mr. Lace that it struck me, like an ax spinning through the center, what I'd done.

*

My brother didn't die in a fire. Though sometimes I tell the story that way. Even when I tell the other story to make myself know it, the truth is not quite the truth no matter how much I need it to be, no matter how much of it I tell. Too many things got lost that afternoon, and the truth can't hold it all.

An accident. A murder. It's been a long time since I've had a brother to drive around the county with, slip along the north banks with. A long time since my brother gave me a story of rescuing, though his voice is in my head. Some things do not die. And a long time, too, since Toadman combed the water with his frog-thumb. I stood with my shoes in the mud, my body so still, waiting for that moment when a frog made a swimming leap out from under a hiding place. Every time one did, it was a miracle. And I was there. A part of it.

2.

The Boobie Trap

—

"Redwoods," Hammond said, "hold this earth together. They never lose the dirt." He stomped at the center of our living room from where he sat in his big easy rocker. The windows got the shakes. He said, "Roots this wide," and opened his arms into a wingspan meant to encompass the stretch of our trailer. It was Sunday, his day off from pulpwooding in the dry-hot, and those wings turned heavy quick. He flopped them down to let them calm. He said the end of his prayer, "A good life for a family out in the redwoods, Chick Pea," and opened his eyes, "Amen."

Our last name is Pea. As the smallest, I got nicknamed Chick, along with Knot on account of the snarls I sometimes get in my hair, and Sapling or Sapling Lulu, depending on his inclination when he calls me to listen.

Momma said from the kitchen bar, "We ain't moving," cause we live just out of Blountstown, which belongs to her.

"You know I'm a passerby, Chick." Which I do. "I come down to lay road under sun." Hammond came from western coal Kentuck. "Hit all the devil spots at night not caring for getting tired. That's how I met your momma at The Boobie Trap," which is something she rather me not know. But this story, like the redwoods, is one he tells so often, I've recorded it deep. I forget what I learn in school, for there's no mystery to words or numbers. They just sit in books like salted slugs. But his stories are words set loose into the air. All I have to do is reach out, pluck them to my bones.

"Hush," Momma said. It was almost one, lunch finished. The three of us had found our afternoon place settings. Momma, the domain of the kitchen, where cooked smell of onion wilted under the AC box, where fork tines got scrubbed back into silver. Hammond and me, our living room, where he'd started to drink the Comfort. The alcohol in him was making him grin.

Hammond said, "She got up on that stage so pretty, I was moved to pick up the wooden blocks they keep on the tables. I drummed them to her dancing like this—" He rapped my knuckles on a nail keg he used for refreshment.

"I like dancing," I said, and he threw my hand. It swung the air.

"Of course you do. You're your mother's child and a Chick Pea Sapling Lulu."

No, I wanted to tell him, *It's not cause I'm all the things you claim. It's cause dancing reminds me of you.* I've seen him tip-toe our trailer without realizing.

Momma dropped a load of silverware onto the bar and did her best huff and jog until she stood in front of Hammond. He was watching a commercial about the super fitness machine with *1-800* flashing and the mute on. "If you don't hush it," she said cause she's been the counter to his good buzz my whole life.

"The light from the tube and the sun off the blinds is putting a shiny coat on you, Rady"—he sniffed both horizons in— "like the nothing you wore when you stepped round that stage, sweating it all—"

"Shut up." Momma turned the TV dark in one click, then she

stared hard at me for the fury in her had switched tracks. "Get on out of the house, Knot. Don't waste a pretty day." Momma did her famous head swoop, a cow hitting flies, to indicate where the door was—I knew where it was. She did not offer to send me to my room cause it's next to our living room with walls hollow as a heart for pressing an ear against.

Hammond said, "Hey, Rady, I just want to say you still got your figure." He rolled his backside down the cushion, then rocked up like he was riding a current of Big Creek. God, he was no help.

Momma stomped and I jumped, but not in time to beat out the good slap she got in, which caused me to tumble-fall into the keg—the wide of our trailer is narrow—and his Comfort spilled, soaked right into his jeans wetting him in sweet orange.

"Shit," he said.

The floor groaned in protest.

"Goddamn it, that's my money wasted," he said.

"Well you shouldn't of been talking, Hammond," Momma said.

"My day off to live how I want, and if you don't like it, you can get on the Devil's road to Hell before I do."

I worried one day he'd put those words to me cause they dwelled in him like California Redwoods. Talk of going was the truest part of Hammond—either he was or someone was. No matter how much spit Momma blew, she was a songbird. But Hammond is thunderclap put in a man, and thunder like that can't be kept in for long.

I was up and out the door before she could get me again. I told my legs to spark. They obliged, tilting me south through Mr. Cashel's forest.

*

We don't have redwoods in Blountstown, but we do have cedars, which appear like shaggy weeds next to the sawtooths and red and white oaks, the gnarled-trunk dogwoods that get blighted by summer, and the sourwoods, sumacs. The sours and feathery macs aren't as tall as I am even though I'm only a sapling. Hammond claims if you bend me wrong, I'll straighten up just like one.

What I really am is a branch-breaker. I tear branches out of their sockets to mark my trails, though, unless the trees are too green and chewy in the tree's armpit to give. Those branches I have to let go of in order to keep on sparking. Meanwhile, low grabbers and briars snag my ankles and make me buckle, which is what happened on that day. I had to stop and suck air inside a round of sawtooths. When the wind finally decided to brush through, my trembling passed, which meant the thunder in Hammond had passed. My stomach unknotted. I straightened myself up.

"Spark, Sapling Lulu, spark," I gave the order. My legs followed the broken branches home.

*

I didn't go directly in. I've learned better than to step into a hornet's nest. So I climbed the hickory at the edge of the yard, up through its leafed camouflage, my palms and shins gumming black with sap. Below, Momma popped from one yellow window to the next, for the pretty day was over and night overtaking. Then she got as low as crickets busy with something on the floor I couldn't see.

It was almost fall. A much needed cool down had yet to happen. This was the time when crickets rubbed their feet and legs into chimes, and their wings into sails, hoping to catch winds far, far south before the first freeze snapped them in two.

I stayed in the hickory clocking time by Momma's bopping. No sight of Hammond. But his truck was there, so he hadn't gone for more Comfort or headed to The Bobbie Trap.

Sometimes, I find him there after he's done with work, after he's thundered at Momma, or when he can't get tired and I want to be near where he is. *I've gotten myself lost again*, he claims. I've asked him why he goes and this is what he tells me.

What I know about that place comes from the one story Hammond tells about Momma, and from what I've seen from outside—The Boobie Trap is less than a mile east through Mr. Cashel's forest. It's a block building painted white with blacked out windows, with inside music loud enough to shake every parked truck mirror. And hotrod cars waxed shiny, waiting for their men that could be my father. Occasionally, painted girls. They appear with more makeup than my mother would ever wear or allow me to. On their bodies, less pretty than a dress. Dancers.

I've looked at Momma to see if any of the painted ones could've been her at one time, but I don't see it. And though I said to Hammond I like dancing, really I'm a branch-breaker. Dancing is silly business. If he ever stops swinging his fingers to the beat in his head, I'll tell him the truth.

I will say some of the girls ain't girls. They're women as old as Momma, coming out front to smoke cigarettes. Difference being—the girls have small bright phones to fidget with and smile into and say *Hey, my baby, hey* to some far off someone. The painted women lean on the building to gain rest, their arms crossed except when taking in smoke.

But Hammond's Ford with its square grill was in the yard, not at The Trap, so he had to be drunk asleep.

I was red-scratched, clinging to branches when my cat Russel clawed up the shellbark next to me and meowed his long curling complaint. The jig was up, so I waded down, slugged through the crickets, in the grass, readying myself for my punishment of being out after dark. School was tomorrow. I *did* have a defense—Momma said for me to get. I done as told. There.

But in the middle of slipping through the screen door, she flung open the white main door and looked at me in such a way I did not recognize her as my mother. The light coming from behind her filled the dark with a gulf of yellow dust I was afraid she'd fall into. I grabbed the railing to steady myself in case she did. I said, "What's a matter?"

"Your father's gone," she said.

I thumbed behind me. "His truck."

"He took the road walking. Said he'd hitch. Said his truck was for us girls now." She put her hand on my shoulder then, as if she'd figured out the path of what to say and do with me. Now she could be herself. My heart ticked up the ladder.

"He'll be back," I said. The man had never left us for long, and he wasn't big on walking since he spent six days a week on his legs clearing timber. Walking for just walking-sake was my domain.

Momma burst a cry. She leaned on me and I stiffened my sapling back. Soon I began to wiggle under the weight of such a heavy fallen branch. We got to the blue rug on the floor—didn't make it to the sofa—and lay in the cat hair cloud and orange spice of the Comfort together. There, I let the blue rug do the holding until we got sleepy.

*

Next morning Jack F come round to collect Hammond for pulpwooding and Momma greeted him. "Hammond's to California. You know how he's always talking about redwoods. Said he's done with everything here, including me and Chick."

Momma started to cry again—the woman can be a blubberer—and I felt sucker-punched. Every time she claimed he was gone for good, I had to fight it.

Jack F switched off his engine, squeaked his door open. It was unlike the smooth swish of Hammond's. Pebbles under Jack F's boots rolled, and I got to my window, turned the lace curtain from the edge just enough. In that small frame, he held up my mother where I'd failed to last night. Jack F didn't say a thing or grunt. Then, after he'd given enough of his time to solace, he peeled her off, squeaked himself back inside his cab and drove past a jut of pines the sun was starting to get over.

She was still out when the school bus whaled into our yard.

"Chick's got a bug," she said to the driver.

My legs stiffened, ready to do a huff and jog and push open the white main door to prove her wrong.

"Ma'am," he said, this driver who uttered so little I did not know his name. I knew the back of his head—curls of brown, thick not thinning—and he kept his bus interior at freezer levels. I knew that, felt that, which irritated me. But I respected his quiet—quiet was a trait you hoped for in a person.

He pulled the chrome door handle shut, and my classmates pressed their mouths and eyes to the foggy windows. Then the bus roughed into gear and humpbacked out, a ride-along-jail going away before I could make good on my threat.

*

Hooky sounds like fun, and I did smile, seeing those faces pressed up like tree frogs on glass, but in general, I don't prefer spending time alone with Momma. Hammond's the one with a sense of humor. He makes the sky lighter. Even if I can't dance, the way he talks and moves is like stepping to time. He's the dancer of us. Just a lightness to him.

My mother is a thud-rock. I guess she's got more shape than a rock—the way Hammond sees her anyway—but she's all about chores and being productive, spending time so busy she doesn't have to think, which is unlike Hammond who thinks often about redwoods. When he talks of them, how they're stronger than any man or anything man has made, tall, so damn tall, telling how we could live as a family among the redwoods and survive on our wits alone, my mother's brain is cued in to the oven timer, the squash casserole browning and the leg quarters broiling. Or she's looking past Hammond to the exercise machine commercial that plays on a loop. The TV people move back and forth on bendable iron chairs for what looks like hours of torture. Even if they're smiling carefree, their bodies are the hands of clocks spinning out of whack. Sometimes Momma follows the edges of the windows, where they meet up to miter, then to where the sun comes through the transparent center. It blinds, so she has to open and shut her eyes until the world gets dark enough and she doesn't have to. My parents' relationship has always been this one-way—Hammond talks; Momma shuts and opens her eyes. She doesn't listen to him anymore, though I'm not sure she ever did. I'm the listener. I'm not saying she's simple cause that wouldn't be fair, but I will say she's holding onto this life where the oven timer is guaranteed at some point to ding to a stop just so she can be reset.

We kept busy—dusting, sweeping, washing, clotheslining, going to Blountstown Mercantile for supplies. I had to scrub the oven clean.

"But it's a self-cleaner," I said in protest.

"That's the easy way out," she said. "And for us girls nothing's easy."

This *us girls* business was starting to chafe.

1. I was a daddy's girl through and through and she knew it. I loved Momma out of duty only. She was a shape made for his hands, not mine, and I didn't want to be around a thud, fall-to-the-ground, rock.

2. She'd never said *us girls* before. She said it as if she had empirical knowledge he wouldn't be back. I believed Hammond would.

But knowledge always wins out over want.

*

For a week I was forced to play hooky so we could scrub the trailer raw. I've never missed the parts of speech so much. I didn't miss my frog-eyed classmates. We hadn't remade our blood-pacts lost over summer. Besides, I don't make friends until they prove their worth.

Then on the following Sunday after his disappearance, Momma's family drove up in the floating caddy—Grandma Tug, Aunt Otha Wayne, Aunt Pat, and Aunt Clytie. The uncles had gone out to hunt with Grandpa Lute. Momma's family were like positive and negative wires on a circuit. Men all ran together on one line, women on the opposite other. Rarely did you spot them together except Thanksgiving and Fourth of July—the two sacred be-together days.

Now that I was almost an adult, I got stuck with my aunts, especially during moments of grief. Grief was the domain of the family women for they had suffered. Aunt Otha had lost two husbands—one to blood cancer, one to a self-inflicted gunshot wound. We were surprised when someone else asked her to take up vows. She was jinxed. Aunt Pat's first husband cut off her left thumb in a fit of rage after she undercooked his frozen duck and got him sick. The uncles ran that one out of town. High blood pressure was the circulating curse of Aunt Clytie. When the pressure got salted and stacked too high, she stabbed herself in a leg to bleed it away. Momma always put knives under sink when Clytie visited. And, she'd never married. Lonesomeness of that kind was unbearable for everyone except me on the sacred be-together days.

The men liked to go hunting to get away from grief. They

got enough of it at home, they said, chuckling. When I was young, I got sent off with them. They thought it cute edifying me about the outdoors, but none of them—let me be clear—my uncles or my aunts, have once wanted to know what I like about nature. I can say for sure, it has nothing to do with cute. If they did ask, I'd tell them the woods are where I feel safe, where I take Hammond's stories to speak out loud just to hear myself in his words while the trees make a cradle for the wind and for me. Otherwise, I keep bottled up, and though Momma stays bottled—I get it honest—her glass breaks when family pulls into our yard.

It was Sunday. Aunt Otha Wayne brought pie.

"Can't have grief without pie," she said in welcome.

Aunt Clytie brought her pecan salad and there was a rotisserie chicken from the store and candied turnips, sausage rolls—foods I can't be around without tearing up. I feel guilty and empty and knotty like my nickname implies even if there's no actual grief, for the essence of that food is sorrow, and to eat it is to bear it inside you.

Our kitchen table was a foldup card, too small to sit around, so we let it hold the food. We fixed our plates, stood quietly to devour in the window sun, then stacked our plates on the bar for washing later. We took to the living room chairs where the air was Pine-Sol clean. We made the circle.

"Your man's not coming back, you sure?" Aunt Otha said, looking for crumbs to dust off her paisley church dress. She sat closest to Momma and was closest to Momma in all ways. Irish twins, only eleven months separated them.

Momma nodded her head. She was in the big easy rocking

slow, crying hard, and I was getting worried. For her crying had rolled in with a whimpering power I wasn't used to, then rolled out, only to come back stronger with the moon getting bigger, and she wasn't one to drink lots of fluids. If she didn't stop, she would dehydrate.

"Well, good riddance," Aunt Clytie said who was my favorite even if a spinster. She was youngest. By the fault of her age and loneliness, Clytie understood me better than the rest of them. Her saying good riddance, however, was a deep strike.

"Amen," Grandma Tug added. "Something was crazy about Hammond. Lute said so." She was the only one dare put on a wife beater and jeans.

"Didn't know how to love you right was all," was what Aunt Pat said who'd taken vows into the unhappiest of marriages. Uncle Tick wasn't a finger cutter, but Aunt Pat had told the circle more than once, *Tick doesn't affect me*. Carried that on her face—makeup couldn't bury it. She was always looking for someone to be unhappy with.

"Amen," everyone said reverent as cows except me for I loved Hammond and the longer he stayed gone, the fiercer that love grew. Though he could be a yell-hellion, he was a hard worker, a proud pulpwooder—*A job*, he noted, *most people spit on*—just to put food on the table and put a roof above, and he loved me, was good to me, kind, he made the sky lighter. Do you know how hard that is to do? I've tried and can't. It's not part of my disposition, but it is in him and that alone in a person makes them good enough to have around. But I didn't dare say any of this. I was outnumbered.

Our trailer ceiling sagged from the extra family weight, and the Pine-Sol caused my tongue to swell and go numb. Then Momma made a rattle so loud my ears panged with hurt. Aunt Pat got up, and she and Aunt Otha held Momma together. The two bookend splints said, "It's going to be all right. You with us. You going to be all right." Grandma Tug said amen.

"Are you okay, Chick?" Aunt Clytie's voice sliced through the blubbering, but when she flapped her shawl arm to put me under wing, I smelled the musk of long-suffering and got out of there.

"He's coming back," I whispered into the gap between us. I couldn't hold my defiant self in any longer, though after I'd spoken, that was all I was willing to say against Momma.

"Of course he is," Aunt Clytie said. She gathered herself into her shawl until she was more cloth than aunt. It wasn't that cool in the trailer. We had the AC box running max, but its breath blowing couldn't compete with the sun. Outside, the trailer's aluminum shell expanded and snapped its rivets.

Grandma Tug scritched chair legs across floor. She lay hands on Momma's head and pulled fingers through Momma's hair. Tug said, "Shhh, now baby," and brushed, "Shhh, my baby girl," brushing lightly down to her daughter's shoulders. Even though it was my momma's hair, all the ache in me stopped, and everyone in that room got quiet in the gulf.

*

I was well into my second hooky week when Momma said she was going out one night.

I stood in front of the white main door with arms crossed. I made the point, "It's us girls, remember?" for she smelled the kind of sickly good that made you want to take a lick, and licking my momma was the last thing I wanted to do. Grape. Momma smelled of grape, which is my favorite. I'll sit near a patch of kudzu in the worst heat just to smell the grape of its bloom.

"We need money," she said, scrubwashed pink and dressed in a dress so flimsy you could tear it off with a finger. "One of us girls has to be a woman. Don't you go anywhere."

I had spent all day in Mr. Cashel's forest searching for a redwood. If Hammond was going anyplace, it was for one of them. *Prettiest trees. So wide*, he told me often, *you can put a car through the trunk*. He had a picture. A postcard of a big yellow sedan inside a hollowed out redwood. The guy and his family sat on the bumper smiling like this was the greatest day of their lives. *Going to see one one day*. He smiled like the man in the postcard and did a jig in his big easy whenever he said that, and I let it wash over me, tickled to see him so happy. You know how it is when someone's good feeling rubs off on you? Later, I dreamed of walking long and stopping at the hollowed out redwood. The yellow car wasn't there anymore, and the tree invited me in. It grew round me a pillow so pithy I lay down and looked up through its center.

"Whatever," I said to Momma. She slapped my cheek bee sting hot. *Whatever* was a word she didn't like.

"Don't make me hit you again."

"What. Ever."

The pink in her cheeks fisted red. "Get out of my way, Knot."

"You going to The Bobbie Trap," I said. It wasn't a question. Something about Momma was what Hammond told in his story. The same look of the painted women I'd seen outside leaning with smoke, needing rest, wearing the same bits of sorrow my aunts wore.

Hammond had a certain smell when he was going there. Not like the rabbit boots of my uncles when hunting, but something similar—an intent. And yet, intent of his kind I knew was just one side needed to make the coin roll.

"Not letting you," I told Momma.

She pushed me to the big easy and hurried outside afraid of I don't know what. Despite my bluster, she was too big for me to take down. Afraid of herself, I decided. First time I'd come across such fear, and I wanted no part.

When the truck's belt whinny become a tiny hum, I stepped into the yard as far as the trailer's dust-light carried. Russel the cat skidded out from under me.

Couldn't smell Momma's grape, but I could smell the gas leak from the big tank out back, which always happened when the wind blew down from north, which it was doing. A front out of Canada had dropped, tangling and untangling the moon from the pines. If Hammond was here, he'd get the ratchet to fix it. Momma wasn't good with tools. Gone anyway, so I had to be the one.

It turned out the flashlight didn't work—dead batteries. I got the ratchet and went on to the tank anyway, lifted the top button, took a whiff. No leak. So I followed the copper gas line under the trailer, wind doing a teakettle whistle, dying back, whistle, as I set my knees atop a rattle of tin that slid sideways. Underneath was Hammond, his mouth open about to say one more thing. Small black bugs crawled out of him, and in places, his skin so blue and tight it cracked. His hands spurred his jean pockets like he'd been placed in a casket proper, but he was on the ground smelling of gas that would only get worse. No mark, no pooled blood on his clothes or the dirt or the tin I could touch or see. And I did not call him up from the dead. I did not cry—enough tears had come from Momma already.

I slammed my fist into the ground.

How did she do it? Kill him?

I brushed the dirt off my knuckles and brushed the bugs off Hammond.

Maybe he did it to himself, thundering so loud.

The only one who knew was her.

*

I broke branches. When a green tender popped up, I smushed it. All I could think, I was proud of myself for not crying when I saw Hammond. It meant I had something tough. And all I could think, I hated myself cause it meant I had something tough. How one thing can make you feel separate—I was split in two. All I could do was keep running full spark until I found the square grill of his truck in the parking lot with the others, the radiator pinging heat, leaking.

"Bitch," I said. I walked up to the door where the big man was. He was always just in or just out under the red door light. Would've taken two of my daddies to make one of him, and he must've seen it on my face, what I come for, cause he said, "No."

"I got someone in there," I said.

He looked away.

"I'm not asking permission," I made things clear.

He said, “Doesn’t matter. You too young,” and crossed his arms. I rooted my shoes in.

The inside music put the concrete under us in a tremor, and we two of us stayed like that until the song stopped. There was whooping, clapping, and the big man said, “Look, if you tell me his name, I’ll try and get him to let go his chair. It’s against the rules, but you youngins keep showing up for your daddies more than I can stomach.”

I almost said Hammond Pea. Stopped myself short cause I had a worry. Might scare Momma to hear the dead called up in her presence. She’d stay in the hole. Almost said her name. Still she’d probably stay. Momma was cowardly—this was proven—which meant I had to catch her unawares.

“That’s all right. I’ll catch him later.” I shrugged and headed into the woods to the back door I knew of from when I walked the perimeter. Though less people used it to come outside, when they did, they paired up to do things in the grass. I preferred to watch the faces of the women in front take smoke, but this door was another way in. So I hid in the cloak of cicadas making the whipcall, crickets putting up sails, and the wind hurrying faster than I’d ever be able to until a man and his girl come out laughing. He pinned the door wide open to the wall, and I bolted.

They were too busy becoming crickets to stop me as I sparked down the hallway. But a new man stepped through the smoke, and the two of us caught the freeze. Behind him a light turned blue like the moon. Everyone started drumming their wood blocks. That racket chipped at my bones. The man, he spaded his hands into his pockets cause I could’ve been his daughter, him figuring out something he didn't like about himself quick. He was an overripe plum, and I stared him down until his shame got fixed onto a speck on the floor. Then a guitar song curled out the speakers overwhelming the wood blocks, and the plum man turned a knob to the bathroom, piss smelling. He shuffled in as apology.

I headed to the moon. Which, turns out, was a stage with dangling colored lights, some of them flashing. On that stage was my mother. She danced how she cooked, stepping from cupboard to oven to fridge to trash to sink trapped in a box, trying to be what she hadn't in a long time. Even if she failed to realize it, she was a ghost in this place just like she was to me. No smile on her, her eyes dull stones in wet mascara. She took off her flimsy dress. She let that grape go, and there was nothing careful about the way she did it. I felt shame for us girls then, shame that I was the one hidden, and she wasn't. To be clear, I've seen my mother naked, just not in front of a bunch of men.

They sat at their tables in work shirts and duckbilled caps, turning the heads of their yellow beer, and then sipping. They were buddied so thick, I couldn't make out the corners of them, couldn't tell if they were laughing at Momma or laughing out of pity. I slipped my foot to the side to slough off the pity I was bearing. I knew too much like my aunts when they set food out for grief. One day their task would be mine.

That thought split me so hard I unstitched, I stumbled. The dark, I tell you, how fast it gets wide, and I could see the hole in the earth people talk of, the one that swallows you and you cannot climb out.

My arms wanted no part of any falling, so they made a truss.

Some things you don't have to do—my hands gripped my shoulders. *Some things you haven't done*—my nails dug in. I hadn't found the redwoods yet, hadn't lost my breath in them, hadn't plucked words from their sky to my bones. I made the promise I'd call the redwoods to listen and tell them Hammond's stories. I would tell them everything that happened. But first, I had a duty to grief.

My hands swiped a block of wood from a table where someone's leather jacket sat drooping off a chair. Through the haze of smoke, the musk and music-talk, the lights curving round my mother's body, my legs sparked to the moon stage. I stood square with its lip and smoothed one edge of the wood down with a finger, cocked it by my ear. I held my body still. The sweat on my skin got hot. And I rosined up. I waited for the switch in her to go off when she would see me clearly.

3.

Shiner

—

Shiner is the lure in the water reeled back. The body of the lure, whether you choose gold or silver—the fish in our pond like gold—catches light in such a way that the light gets pushed down to the deepest parts of the pond. Cold, deep places where normally light can't get to. Just that fleck and fleck along with the hum of the tiny propeller off the lure's nose is enough to draw a fish—I'm talking about a giant bass under the pine roots left to rot when the pond was built. Way before I come into this world or Leafygirl. Back when Grandbaby was a baby.

And now that summer's close to happening, I come to the pond after school every day, fling the shiner out, reel it back again and again until up a giant bass surges toward my lure strong, doing everything it can to put the light and hum in its belly. But none of what the fish does—how fast it shake-rise-pushes against the green water with its rainbow scales, how unthinking it is, never questioning what it wants to get, it just gets—none of it is based on smell like how my dog Bolt-Out-of-the-Blue puts his nose to the wind to figure a corner of the yard worth running through.

No, to these giant bass, it's all shake and rise and take the sun out of the water. For the shiner is a piece of the sun to them, or the moon if you choose silver, fallen into their world. Us humans would have to examine such a piece close up. Give it the eyeball test. We'd want to understand the alien rock first. Fish, they just want to eat. All things get eaten eventually. All things small. Even us once the sun turns cold and the black holes start pulling us to God.

Up top above the water and underneath the sun, planes on their way to B town, an hour south of here. Silvery planes with calm white tails. Unless the wind starts to zig and zag those tails about. Then on the water, we get a rush of tiny waves, and through the pine needles, a shushering. Some of the pines are older than Grandbaby, who is my grandfather. But everyone calls him Grandbaby after all these years cause he's still got a baby's face with snowy tufts of hair along his jaw line, which one day I'll have. He has a bald chin where lightning struck him once, he claims. And he's wide as the trunks of the biggest pines, his legs fatter than taproots. Makes it hard for him to get around. Still he manages. Grandbaby was Leafygirl's father—she got her nickname while flitting about in a dress after church one day, happy just to be a leaf swept up in the wind. That was before I was born. Leafygirl was my mother and drowned herself in our pond where she and I swam and fished.

I think about where she is—the pinpoint spot—cause they didn't dredge her body up. Tried to, but couldn't find her with the chain and hook. Probably her foot's tucked under a stump. They didn't drain the pond cause it's on a spring, cause it's twenty-too-many-acres to pump out, and Blount County doesn't have the kind of money to find a lost woman is how Sheriff Pinkie Sligh put it.

"I tell you Grandbaby, Leafygirl might not even be in your pond," Sligh said, trying not to look at the man laid out on the bed like an unliftable stone. This was after the dredging had failed. Grandbaby refused to get up. All week, he wept and slept, and I had to feed him, had to change the bedpan.

"She could've just left y'all." Pinkie glanced at me when he said that, his face, what part got left out of his hat's shadow, was as pink as his name. This was early November before the first cold snap hit. "What if she swam clear across?"

And got away, I was thinking. What if she got away?

Our pond is full of underground caves, and she fell into one of them, that's what Grandbaby said. He saw her swimming. He watched her from his window. It's the same window Grandbaby watches me from when I fish, so he knows I'm all right. *You all I got now, Tadpole*, he says when I come into his room. I got my name by going to the water.

"I watched her go," Grandbaby said to the sheriff. "She swam way out until her head was just a turtle peeking up. There." He stretched his pointing finger to the X he had fixed in his mind. X marks the spot. And Sheriff Pinkie Sligh walked over, put his hands on the sill, pressed down to hold himself up. He leaned and looked, trying to follow the line of that finger to its end.

"You sure she wasn't angry about something?" He scratched at his chin.

"No. That's where she was. Then she wasn't. Just swam to her own grave. But she didn't mean to do it." Grandbaby dropped his hand, shivering. And I wrapped his hand in both of mine, his skin rough, a bit chilly, my skin the blanket, until he calmed and warmed and Sheriff Pinkie Sligh shut all the doors he had come through and left us. After Thanksgiving, Grandbaby went into town to cash his check. He returned home with Mae.

"She drowned herself," Mae said, who is sixteen and older than me and smarter than me, and the one who talks about such things, all things. "Leafygirl gave up on this life and gave up on you."

"Why she want to give up on me?" I was her only child.

"Couldn't take living," Mae said. She lit a cigarette. One ended. Another began. "Couldn't take it. You'll see."

I wanted a definition of the *it*, which Mae wouldn't give. Her parents had made her quit school to help us. They needed money, and Grandbaby had the Air Force pension. He's one of the few in the county with steady cash. A first Iraq War vet. *Government owes*, he says. *Now they going to pay*. I get money when I knock green pinecones down and sell them ten dollars a bushel at Tugbail's store. But that's just for a month in the fall.

"Sixteen is when you're sweet," she said. "So you better take advantage of my sweetness."

I'm twelve is all. Leafygirl drowned at twenty-nine. Mae's sixteen sweet. And Grandbaby is timeless. He'll live on forever. He says Leafygirl's drowning is just the latest tragedy in his life.

But I like to think when I throw out the shiner, like I'm doing now, the light turning in the water, that my mother catches the light, too, that there is something in her called up—whichever cave she's in or root she's under—that the shiner makes her want to come to it cause she knows the sun off the lure is also me. But nothing comes back from the dead. I told myself this all winter just as I tell myself now.

*

I walk up the hill after not catching, and Mae's on the porch,

Bolt-Out-of-the-Blue slumped next to her on the old boards.

"Why you out here battling mosquitoes?" I say.

"Cause they easy to kill," she says and slaps one. "Your grandfather . . ." she stops, shakes her head. "He don't pay me enough for what he wants."

"He needs somebody to take care of him's all," I say.

She chuckles. "He wants extree. Always wanting a little something more of me. Where's your giant fish, Tadpole?"

"Didn't pull one." My bucket's rattling two shiners with a pair of nose-pliers, and my reel line is clipped bare to the rod. "I saw two giants swimming round each other close to the bank."

"Sweeping tails," Mae says and lights a cigarette. "Fucking." She says it where I almost don't hear, but I do, and she must notice the sheep look on my face cause her feet start to tap. She's barefooting—what Grandbaby calls it—how Mae's left and right foot step and stir the air, drum the boards. She watches them move. She's not watching me any longer, and Bolt gets up off the porch with the same disposition Leafygirl had when preparing supper, not wanting to encourage such rambunctiousness.

All the lights in the house are on it's so dark. Squares of yellow come through the windows and the doorway screen. Still spring enough for the nights to cool. Nothing cooking. Nothing I can smell. Mae was waiting on my catch. And I know what the word means, the one she said. I hear people say it in a nasty way, or a harsh way, all the time. But I don't really know it. Not like I do *eat* or *catch* or *burn*. I have felt those words in my gut and my hands. What Mae said, that word is just a word.

"I was your age," she explains, "first time I got swept up by someone. I can show you, if you want."

"That's all right," I say uneasy.

"Well you ain't like Grandbaby." She shifts around in her chair, pulls at her blue dress with the brown edge, which makes the cutout along her neckline into a tidy collarbone square. "That man's the horniest thing. I don't know how Leafygirl took it."

"She didn't," I say.

"Hm," Mae says and starts barefooting again, looking down. "Sometimes people know things they can't admit to. And they can live that way for a while. One day you'll get your feet right." She stomps to a stop. Draws her cigarette tip hot red. Bolt-Out-of-the-Blue barks at her.

"Shhh," I say and whip his speckled hide with the end of my fishing rod. He yelps and runs to the front of the house where the truck's parked.

Mae says, "I don't mean anything. No harm between us. I like you, Tadpole."

*

Next day I'm throwing the shiner out, reeling, throwing. The fish won't bite. They're too busy fucking, I guess. Sure enough, two of them are in the shallows with fishtails swinging clock-hand up, clock-hand down. They move like they might switch into a water moccasin if they keep at it.

I put the lure where the giants are, but they don't mess with it, so I put my hand in the water cause they have a mouth like a scrub brush—that's what Leafygirl said once after catching a five pounder—“Giants are without real teeth.”

Then, “Come here, Tadpole,” Leafygirl called me to her. She hinged the large mouth open by way of her thumb strapped over its bottom lip, her fist tucked under its wet white chin. “It can’t hurt you,” she said and I locked my hand onto hers.

Now, I just want to grab one, not get fin-stabbed. But the water is too mossy to see into, and I’m doing more feeling than grabbing. They just sway around my ruddering hand like it isn’t there, like I’m part of what’s going on, too. Scales brushing, tickling, rough and slick in cool mud water.

Then their world gets quiet and they’re gone.

*

“I put my hand in,” I tell Mae that night.

“In what?”

“The giants swimming round.” I swirl my hand down.

“What it feel like? Tell me.” She’s making fried potatoes and the last of the venison steaks, what Brother Wilson brought when Leafygirl died.

“I just—my heart knuckled up.” I thump my chest bone. “Then a string got pulled through me, tight. That’s what it felt like.”

She nods. “When it’s good it feels that way.”

“What happens when it’s not good?”

She flips the meat in the oil slow like she doesn’t enjoy doing it anymore. Some questions shouldn’t be asked. “You feel dull,” she says. “Leaves you feeling dull is all.”

Grandbaby never eats with us, so Mae takes him food, and

afterward, after I've been in bed awhile, I creak open my door, slow-step it to Grandbaby's door. They don't hear me. Can't. They're too busy making the air whoop and moan.

When she first got here, Mae slept on the couch. Same thing Leafygirl done when we arrived from Piedmont, and Grandbaby took us in. Before then, we were in the foothill towns, switching out of motels into trailers. *You here for good this time,* he said to Leafygirl. She squeezed the bones in my hand. Eventually, just like my mother, Mae snuck into his room.

The whoop and moan pitches into a fierce growl. The string through my body pulls and pulls. Then the growl snaps in two, and Mae's left crying.

"What is it?" Grandbaby says. "What's wrong girl. Shhh." It's all soothing he's doing with his voice. Grandbaby is a smooth baritone, he claims, and I've heard him. He's right. His voice sounds like taking your finger down a silk shirt from collar to tail. He did church solos for a time. "Wouldn't that good?" he says.

"You take good care of me," Mac says, trying to mend her breathing. "But I don't want you to."

"What you mean you don't want me to?"

"I want to be on my own," she says. "I don't want to fuck a man fifty years older than me."

Nothing else gets said, and I get down to the rug where the crack beneath the door is, where their voices stir the dust.

Then, "You don't like me?" he says, a cold thundering. "You don't want to be with me?" He's shuffling uncomfortable in his king sheet I can tell. "Get out. I'll find somebody else. Go. Somebody who wants what I am and what I got."

“No. Please, Grandbaby,” she says, “don’t turn away. Sometimes I say the truth of what I’m feeling a little too loud. I’m grateful to you. My parents never took care of me this good.”

“I’m good for that,” he says. “I take care. All I am, maybe.”

“You more than that,” she says. “I promise.” And his body must’ve turned, again, cause they’re kissing or she’s kissing his wide back that’s always hurting, something calm like the sound of brushes brushing, and the sniffling and the crying done.

*

I dive down into the pond. It’s the day before the last day of school. All the other kids fidgeted in their seats before the final bell, chomping at the bit like horses for summer—*We’re going to have fun*! Like summer could be plucked up easy by the handful, and, if held tightly enough, never let go of.

I swim to the bottom, sift my hands through the mud, hoping to find Leafygirl, trying to do what the chains and hooks couldn’t. But I cannot bring her up. Just pebbles, and slick branches, and a gurgly bottle of beer. Grandbaby used to toss in his beers, but he won’t come to the water since she drowned. All the time I’m diving, Bolt’s on the shore barking for me to come to him. He doesn’t like water—makes him seasick to get in. Turning old has made Bolt this way.

“Get out of there,” Mae says. She’s on the bank patting his neck so all Bolt can do is whine. And I do what she says.

First thing, she slaps me. Hard. “Don’t drown on me and leave me with Grandbaby.”

"I was just looking for Leafygirl." The hot sting swirls and pricks a whole circle of my face numb.

"She's gone."

I start to tell something about what I heard last night. I start to tell her to take it back what she said about Leafygirl, but two giants are rolling up the bank.

"Going on beds," Mae says. "They put their babies there."

I tell her to follow me, and she does. I take her hand.

"What you doing?" She yanks back.

"Nothing bad," I tell her and hold her hand, again, smooth it, and put hers in the cool water with mine where the giants are turning round. They bump against us, whack us with their tails and slide across our fingers. Bolt-Out-of-the-Blue wants to get in. He roots his paws at the edge—that's all he's willing to venture. We tell him to shush whenever he growls out a bark.

"Such a good feeling," Mae says and laughs, "which I ain't had in a while. Lord," she says, "thank you."

"You're welcome," I say in my deep God voice, which is deeper even than Grandbaby's baritone. She slaps my face but lighter, and we giggle louder.

*

That night after supper, after I've tried to fall asleep and can't, Mae slips out of Grandbaby's room and gets underneath my covers behind me and puts her arm over me.

"I still want to go to school," she says.

"Last day is tomorrow," I say. "Too late this year."

"I still want to go."

"Then go," I say, "in the fall." I snuggle in to her. If she'll let me, I'll teach her how to catch fish with a shiner.

Mae shakes her head, rubs her nose against the back of my neck. She smells of white smoke and sweat. "Got to take care of Grandbaby. My folks need the money. I need the money. The extree he give. I've never had a place and I do here. Don't say anymore," Mae says. "Just want to hold you and feel what it's like, someone going to school. It's a good feeling to have when someone you care about has what you want, and you can let a little rub off onto you."

I try to be quiet, let her rub. "What will you do with the extree?" I whisper.

"Get far away from here."

"What about me?" I say.

"I'm not taking you," she says.

"Leafygirl didn't take me with her either." And the string that had pulled from my stretched out toes to the top of my head, and the warmth my back felt leaning against Mae—everything vanishes. I try to get out. Mae pulls me to her tight.

"Leafygirl couldn't take you to the place she went," Mae says. "That was her struggle. I'm the one needs you now."

"I'm not yours," I say and pull harder till I'm loose and hurrying off the bed.

She says, "Wait," but that word is no good either, and she flips onto her back, crosses her arms. She gazes at the edges, the center, the whole wide-length of the ceiling. Slowly, she opens her arms to breathe. The blankets are about halfway, and there's enough of a moon to see her breasts, smaller than Leafygirl's. Her collarbones lift, fall, lift. "You're right," she says, all dull. "You are your own."

Part of me wants to snuggle up, except I can't figure where to place my body cause it's just Mae and the moon and not me now. I'm not invited here.

So I creak open my door, shut it, slow-foot my way into Grandbaby's room. He's snoring out black air, and the room smells like his bedpan smells. He's on a pill from the doctor. He won't wake up.

I lift the window.

Out there is the pond. Enough of a moon to make the water into a flat blue field. I try to find the line Grandbaby pointed Sheriff Pinkie Sligh toward, that X where Leafygirl is now. If I could, I'd peel away the water, every layer, like blankets pulled off a bed, until I saw Leafygirl and all the flecks shiners steal from the sun and send down.

My mother lived quietly. We never had a TV cause she didn't want one. Used to at night, the two of us sat on the couch where she held me. This she did after opening the door, so all the sounds—crickets in the fall, toads in spring, the pines and their shushering—carried through the screen to us. Her arms would be around my shoulders crooked and loose, and me quiet with her, too, my arms around her belly and back, not wanting to go to bed, not wanting to go free just yet cause always between not wanting one thing and not wanting another is the fear of wanting. But if I could, I'd peel back every layer of water, I'd gather up every fleck and bone and shell and stick down in the caves and let them burn me, cut me, make me shiver. Then I'd put them all back where they should go.

Baby Forever

—

Every night, there's no place to go. No one to go back for. Had a home and a girl that wanted me cozy and still, but that craziness could only last for so long. Off I went, driving to B town, up and down its iron ore hills, past its rich houses that bleed onto the poor ones, hospitals, skyscrapers, airport in blue lights. All the way to the old factory squares in the north end that stay broken out and spray-painted on. They were the places our fathers and uncles dreamed up to make a secure life, where our mommas wrapped us in skin and bone and pea shells desiring pearls. Now they're fort ruins with nothing left to protect, where I dreamed I was a bucking horse no one had the hands to break. But how long can someone drive before they pull into a ditch, fall so far down they die, their momma singing from above, "Don't sleep, my baby, forever."

I stay out of the ditches by circling houses of people I don't know. Sometimes they come to the window to stretch or drink tea or out onto the porch to sweep it. Maybe, when I saw you there, you wondered who I was passing. Or maybe, you had been me at one time, restless and wandering, too. Most nights, all I find are lit up squares of chandelier glass light, and further in, a funky red art poster, the top of an old dresser, the back of a chair watching the stairwell spiral because everyone has been eaten up by the light. Everyone has become what the TV watches, the refrigerator hums at, the dog barks and barks and barks until I end up at the Hangout Lounge where you appear, demanding a kiss.

"Stolen," I say and point to your ring. "Who's the thief?"

"Gone," you say. "He and I—I wear it to remember we had a past. What was yours like?"

When I talk of the factories and my own tattered skin, it sounds like coughing, which turns you off. You can't get into, you say, fucking a man who talks about his past with a stutter.

So I go and drive and steer until the truck feels as if it will never touch this earth again. It's like that, too, when you finally give yourself away. "Please," you say, "kiss me with what our parents desired."

Has to be an end to what's going on in me. We drink and kiss and fuck until we break the sky apart. By morning the sky is put back together, washing over all we undid, and by night I'm driving round your house. Eventually, you'll call the police so you can disappear to some other man, give him everything that is nothing of you at all.

Sometimes it's not the yellow window glass I see or the downtown with its tall empty buildings coming into view from over the hills, or the factory docks made of dead horses. Sometimes there's a lightning storm, those crooked sticks of summer, ready to take the spit out of my throat and make it into rain. Before passing, I beg the storm to take me, catch me in the wind like strewn paper and haul me off. But it won't. It just can't. The ditches, they get wider, deeper, full of new water and night. The road, it narrows. From below you sing, “Come now, my baby, you can’t drive forever.” You promise to rock me until what is in me stops. “Fall like this,” you say before you place my hand over your heart.

Asleep in Peggy's Grace

—

What I did was put Peggy Grace in a box. But her current was sweeping fast—she busted my box quick—and all I could do was run along her bank to try and fish my box out.

Peggy's not Big Creek, mind you, but when the rain cut down the sky, her water refused to trough, and that's why I went in the rain to box Peggy Grace—protect my valley home. She had a separate mind. Didn't care what I wanted, and neither did Honey.

"Ras, we have to shake a leg," Honey called from inside her car.

My valley home is Honey's garage. She took me in after I escaped my kin—this was from a long time back. What I have now is Peggy Grace Creek and Honey and the fields round us and where I sleep and my government check for food, though it's hard dealing with Tugbail, moving through the line at his store. Once, when I got a T-bone, Tugbail put it back in the cooler instead of checking it out, upset, like I'd grabbed that bone straight out of his gut.

"Like you get to choose," Honey said and stomped to the cooler. She got the bone, put it back on the line. "You going to let him make the purchase," she said.

Tugbail chewed his lip cause he's all rubber. "Ain't right," he said. "He ain't right, and you, well—"

"Don't look at me unless you want to get slapped." She

leaned her fists on the line. Her eyes made the fire. He looked to the shopping buggies outside the doorway—empty. Beyond them the one tree. Above, the blue.

This kind of thing had me in a twitch, but Tugbail just withered.

"Ain't right," he said softer, shaking his rubber head. Then he rung up the bone, and I cooked that one special. I tell you, Tugbail wouldn't care if this rain took me to somewhere else. Just Honey.

"Ras," she called again. The passenger door was open and the rain was beating a hop off the cab. I almost slipped into Peggy Grace sweeping faster than I could run. My box was far, far—

"Now!" Honey hit the horn. That sound clicked in me, and I mudded up the bank, took my place in the seat. I closed the door. She sighed.

"Don't you understand Peggy's in a fury? You fall in, I can't get you out."

"You'd come," I said.

"Ain't got the strength."

"Oh, you would," I said, dog-shaking my shirt. But there was no flicking off the wet.

"Wouldn't." She made that word crystal and pushed the gearshift with the heel of her hand. The transmission scratched until it caught.

I was so busy with the box, I forgot to pack a thing. If they was gone when we returned, my things, they gone! I told Honey this, laughing like I was full of the lightest snow.

"You'll regret such a wish," she told me and up we went to the high ground place.

*

The high ground place had water but no food. A woman said, "None till morning. We're in a crisis. Find you a spot on the floor." She gave a blanket, a bottle of water, and Honey and I stepped over bodies till we got to a clearing and lay and stared at the ceiling. Nothing dripped through like it did in Honey's kitchen. Oh, we could hear the rain making a beat to the flickering light. We could hear someone cough. Someone hooted the owl and Honey answered. She gave us all her long weep.

"Wipe them tears," I said, which is what she says to me whenever I swell—*Buck up, Ras, you're a man*, she says. *Weeping never done a soul any good. People do it after the fact of things and much too late.*

She couldn't hear them words now.

"I don't want to lose my home," was what she said instead. "Only thing that's mine and no insurance."

"It's rundown." The tin garage I slept in was newer. It come out of a kit.

"But it's mine. I grew up there. What I got all of."

"I'm hungry," I said.

"You're breathing."

"Not enough to just breathe. I want food," I said.

"Shhh." She rubbed her tears into my arm. "You get too loud, they won't let you stay."

So I shut eyes and thought of the box. Not what happened—it busting in Peggy Grace's current—but what I intended, which was to push the box down to the bed, hold it there until every curl of water purled inside. Then I would hoist Peggy Grace up onto a shoulder and carry her and keep her next to me sloshing on high ground until she grew so still the rain above us stopped. I would carry her down, no matter how heavy, then open the lid and pour her back onto her bed.

*

Next morning the church people come in with armloads of food, every Christian giving the heaven smile, so glad to see us. God bless, people will feed you in a crisis, especially these ones from Sky Ball, our saviors.

We got an allotment and I gulped my chicken, coleslaw, roll. Honey let me have what she couldn't eat, which was most of it. Then we went back to our blanket. I put my hand on Honey's leg.

"Wish we could do some things."

She shook her head. "Can't with all these people. And I don't want to. That's just crazy." Her body moved off until I was touching the sweat-freeze of the cement and not her.

I started to put my hand back just to rub gentle, but she didn't want that either. The stares the people made kept prying me. On the blanket, Honey's leg doing the twitch. And everything in me dropped below zero what the food had made warm.

*

Blanket or no blanket that floor's hard. On the fifth day, I said, "I want to see my valley home."

"Calm down, calm down," the woman in charge said. She was from Birch Springs, that clear water place, and thought she was the boss of all. Her nametag was a list. "Sorry you're uncomfortable, Sir. Here, take a second pillow."

"Don't want your pillow."

"Ras," Honey called. She rolled the bottom of her shirt in her hands like she does when she's about to take it off and let me in.

In the night, I dreamed the squeezed-in bodies spun through the air. The trunk of me was the axle, my legs and arms the spokes spinning every body until my calves knotted and fell and I woke up dizzy. Could hear the rain make the dark darker. Knew Peggy Grace was still spilling out of her trough. The room swam but without the floating bodies I was afraid of. Had to breathe in and out until I was sure Peggy's current hadn't come this far up and my cramps were gone. Then I eased myself back into sleep.

Now it was morning, the rain lulling. Honey said, "Ras," this second time low and sweet. I followed to where she was and sat down.

"I need you." She got in close and put my hand up her shirt so my arm rested between the bluffs of her breathing and no one could tell what was going on. I could smell her sweat.

"Why?" I said.

"You shouldn't ask for the good things you get. I don't ask why I get to have you."

"That's easy," I said. "You found me walking the road. Now there's you and me and Peggy Grace and nothing else." Which is what she tells me when she lets me in and we're holding each other after and she starts to sing, *Once lost, now found,* like we might fall off the tick if she doesn't.

She sighed. "The water's taking this world, Ras."

"You don't know that," I said. I did not tell what I dreamed of.

"I know," she said.

*

She was right on half—the water took some. My work boots were tangled in a big upturned chinaberry with feathery sumac and ribbons of tin and stacked up branches and cemetery flowers downstream. I used those boots for kicking up Idahos, for mowing grass, for squatting off the bank to sway mussels loose. The ribbons of tin were my valley home, what Honey let me have when she picked me for her—how long ago was it when she did that? And who were the people I left behind I keep forgetting? Honey wasn't using the garage except for storage, so I pushed her boxes into a bird's nest.

The water didn't sweep away her home, which was given to her when her mother died. Honey's father had owned the valley and Peggy Grace, too. He made tomatoes, cotton, cattle. He plowed light into dirt until a stroke. Honey's mother sold everything except the house and the acres to Peggy Grace. Had to sell. Now the house was thicked with mud..

Could not be lived in until fixed, the agent said. He thudded shut the front door, tacked up a notice, and came to where we stood on the steps. He handed Honey some papers.

"Where we going to live right now?" Honey wanted to know.

"You'll have to figure that yourself. Family?"

She shook her head.

“Neighbors?”

“Them.” She scuffed her boot. “Don’t you see what I’ve been dealt?”

“You got me,” I said.

“Can’t turn to you.”

But I swelled up big enough to lift us from this world.

“You’ll get sick if you go in that house now. Wind up in a hospital. The churches and the government will be over to help. They’ve promised.” The agent nodded and leaned from the steps towards his car. He cranked up and was gone.

The sun was out good. Peggy Grace was running calm in her trough. I said, “Everything’s going to be all right,” echoing the sun and the water and the man’s promise made. But Honey walked in, let the door close. She turned the lock.

“You can’t do that,” I said.

Her feet went padding, then her sound switched to quiet.

I struck the door with a fist. “Let me in, let me in.” I slung my shoulder until I busted through.

Downstairs, silt stuck to the walls, table, chairs, the floor, and when I put my hand on the purple sofa, water poured up. So I went up the stairs stomping, calling. She wasn’t in the rooms. So I took the ladder to the attic where the musty smell of insulation was and not fish and mud. By the window was Honey sitting in a curl. When I touched her, she kicked back.

“Ouch,” I said.

“Ouch is right. This is too big a mess to fix. And I don’t have money,” she said.

"Someone's coming to help. We'll be okay."

"You think they coming, Ras? Really?"

"The agent promised, so—"

"People like him promise a lot they don't mean."

"What we going to do then?"

She said, "What you going to do and what I'm going to do are separate questions. I can't carry you anymore."

"But you found me. Picked me out," I said.

"No one will let us live with them together, Ras."

"I can live in their garage," was all I said, though I meant to tell how I didn't need carrying.

"They won't let you," she said.

"You let me in yours."

"That was—" She didn't finish.

"Someone's coming to fix it," I said. "I don't know how to make you believe."

"You can't. If I thought there was a way, I'd let you in, Ras, I promise, but I don't and that's what matters here."

We were in the corner of things—me in one and her in the far other. Sunlight came through the middle of the glass. Outside Peggy Grace sweeping slow. Honey kept drawing away, taking tinier breaths, and I was afraid she'd quit taking them at all, afraid the light would slip back on itself until there was none. I was already full of dark I didn't want, so I got up, walked the ladder down, the stairs down past the grass and briars that were whipped.

I got to the thick mud shore and looked back at the attic glass—the sun hit it so bright the glass seemed to turn to tin. The sun so warm, I waded out to the big sleeping stone I go to when I finish my work. I lay there wet and Peggy Grace didn't make me move, didn't pry me. And I didn't feel Honey when she waded out to put her arm around, except the shivering I was doing calmed. The stone became as warm as the sun then, and I put my hand in like a fishtail rudder to guide us downstream. Later, when I wiggled to get closer to Honey, I fell off and bit on water so cold I jumped up hooting the owl. I waited for Honey to hoot me back, but the dark was the one that echoed. Then the stars come to swim Peggy Grace. They dove and dove and wouldn't stop.

Where the Stars Fall Together

—

They make a pool of silver, unstitch the sky, and sift through the pine branches whose needles shake off stars like a dog's fur shaking off bathwater. And still the stars fall. What pieces we catch we hold like thread, whiskey, chigger bites, sin, and we lose like water turning round and round our fingers, like someone's hair we can no longer touch, like the last bits of light mapped on the floor until worn blind-through, sleepless, breath-rattled, we are left to lope through the woods alone.

Wanting a Lover Man

—

Some people never stop talking, and that was, I am certain, the main problem with Bubba. Every morning round nine a.m. he came into Mrs. Holtin's Supermarket and sat down in the rocking chair next to the bug sprays and nail polish remover. For the entire day, he just sat and sat with a gallon of water that he brought from home. That jug had a dirty ring around it you could tell was on the inside, and he sat, swigging and talking until six p.m., which often got pushed up to five even though on the door it says six, cause Mrs. Holtin didn't want to spend that extra hour with Bubba.

Mrs. Holtin is alone these days. Her husband had his heart attack when they went out to the Grand Canyon. He saw it, said, "Mother fucker," muttered those words, croaked them, and grabbed his chest as if his wallet was missing. That's what I hear from Mrs. Holtin's boy, Cecil. He's told everyone this story about his father. He delights in telling it the drunker he gets, snatching at his own chest, making the croak over and over cause the drunker he gets, the more he can't remember what he's said. One night he said my name at least fifty times. I counted them. Fifty times at the beginning of some question—Judy? Judy? Judy?

"What damn it?" I finally snapped back cause there is nothing worse than a man stuck on his own tongue, unsure of what to do next. Well, that's Cecil. He's only sober during the hangover hours—the time, his mamma, Mrs. Holtin, is at work from eight until six, used to be five on the account of Bubba. She didn't like to be in the store with Bubba any longer than she had to. Nobody did cause of all his talking—talk, talk, talk. Talk to anybody about anything.

He'd go off on the importance of nice dress shoes on Sunday, why Vidalia onions were no better than regular onions, and oceans that he'd never seen. Then he'd tell about the countries at the end of those oceans, and pretty soon he'd start rambling on about the people in town. He had a nickname for all of us, and if it wasn't bad, he'd tell it to your face.

Some of the bad ones were like what he called Mrs. Holtin—Mrs. Big Hair—on account of her hairdo being so big. Nice ones were like what he called me—Young Lady—cause I'm young, he said, and a lady.

The last time I saw him was a week ago. That's when he started talking to me about how many blues there were. How each one was kinda lighter or darker than the one you saw before.

"Look at the sky," he said, pointing outside the merchandise window.

"Now look at your paints," he pointed down. He meant to say pants, but his face clamped down on his mouth, causing his wrinkled jaws to flare into gills.

"Now you go look at anything in this store that's got blue on it," he said, "and you'll see what I talk about." He rubbed the bristles on his chin, satisfied that he had told me the most profound thing, a secret to the universe no one else had caught on to, had ever understood.

Tints, I wanted to tell him. *Hues*. Let him know there were-names for all of this, and that he hadn't discovered them. He wasn't the only one with eyes. But I didn't say a thing. I had known Bubba too long not to let him get his way.

So slowly I turned my head from aisle to aisle.

"I see what you mean," I said.

We nodded to each other.

Whenever Bubba got to talking fast and muttering and spitting like retread tires coming off a truck, his language sounded more archaic than Chaucer. Mr. Ribbons, who works at the community college in Snead thirty-five miles away, said so.

Bubba said he knew Chaucer. Met him at Billy's Liquor once and they got drunk together. Whenever Mr. Ribbons came in, Bubba would ask, "How's my friend Chaucer doing?" Mr. Ribbons would stand there, something to buy held quietly in his hands, and he'd give Bubba an obliging smile. Mr. Ribbons is more than just educated. He always wears long sleeve, starch-collared shirts though the weather hovers around a hundred most days of the year. He has a studying look. He comes into Mrs. Holtin's and studies things—Dixie water cups, ingredients in sugar, varieties of ice cream for his wife who's expecting. And Mr. Ribbons, like all of us, took time out from Mrs. Holtin's selections to study Bubba. He said to Bubba, "You're more archaic than Chaucer," who is, by the way, a great English writer. He never hung out at Billy's, I am certain. I remember something about a wife taking a bath and Chaucer when I was in school. But I've been out for two years.

I'm the head cashier over at the Mustang Stop on weekends. That's the only gas station, part-time convenience store in town. It's right next to Mrs. Holtin's. During the week, I hang out with Missie, the other cashier, and help her pump gas. But she's got a flaw. She's a few years younger than me, and you know how high schoolers are, even if she's dropped out. So I take about as much of that giggling and boy-crazy gossiping as I can, then I go next door to check on Bubba.

That day when he was talking about blues, I had purchased some chocolate chip cookie dough ice cream cause nothing beats raw cookie dough.

He was saying you couldn't, even if you wanted, make two of the same color blue. "That's a truth, Young Lady. A fact."

Like I said, my nickname was Young Lady and whenever he added that to his talking, I straightened up my shoulders like my mamma tells me I should be doing all the time cause here I was, this Young Lady, with all this respect being given me, and I wanted to look the part.

"A fact." He smacked his lips dry and swigged another swallow. The water hadn't gotten below the brown ring yet.

Usually Bubba moved onto some other topic, but he had said *fact* about three other times during his *blue* talk.

I could tell he was going to rattle on, so I slipped out the front door, licking a drizzle of ice cream from the side of my half pint, and I was walking and licking to the point that I didn't see it, almost ran into it—Cecil's truck.

"Get in," Cecil said. He spat something at the floorboard.

"I ain't talking with you," I let him know up front and turned the other way.

"Get in," he said louder and rammed one of the gears into its socket, easing the clutch back to make the gear grind.

"I'm still hurting," I said.

"So," he said, refusing to look at where I pulled up my shirt. There was a purplish-black splotch like a dent above my bellybutton.

"I ain't talking with you," I said.

"Come on, Judy." He spat again at the floorboard, then pulled at his hair as if his head was in pain.

This hangover of his must be a bad one, I decided. I was glad about that. His face was sweaty and he was antsy. It was hot, and we both stuck to where we were while the truck idled.

I looked up at the sky. Blue. I wondered if I took a picture of today's sky and tomorrow's sky and showed them to Bubba would he believe, "See Bubba. There is the same color twice." Or would he be right? Would tomorrow's sky be different?

"Judy . . ."

That was all the apology I was going to get—Cecil saying my name half way softly.

The mosquitoes were under the trees cooling it, as Bubba would say. They wouldn't come and bite me, it was so hot.

I waited a little longer.

Then I got in.

That was around 2:30.

Immediately, I noticed a beer in Cecil's hand.

"Feeling better, I see," I said, dipping into my ice cream—it was already liquidy all the way around the part where it touched the carton.

"Doing all right," he said. He was watching the side of Tucker Road, waving to whoever came whizzing by in the other lane. I don't think he really looked at them. Cecil was more interested in wheel rims and paint jobs than people, but waving was habit.

I dug deeper into my ice cream. The cookie dough parts were little round pieces. They must've come from a tube, like the Pillsbury kind in the milk section. His truck, even though it's old, runs good—there's just enough putter in it to settle my stomach. And the more my stomach settled, the more ice cream I stuffed in, and the more comfortable I felt.

*

Cecil parked the truck, kept that stuff in his mouth, spitting a path to the front door of his mamma's house. I followed him, laying my empty half-pint on the steps before I did, licking my sticky fingers.

He didn't say anything as he walked past the kitchen, past the dining room where Mrs. Holtin has a picture of the Grand Canyon framed. The caption underneath says, *The World's Most Breathtaking View*. Bubba said he had been there.

"Yes, yes, Young Lady, it is beautiful. Just an empty hole in the ground—had several people tell me that, but I didn't bother with them. Cause it's not the . . . the . . . hole part, it's the way it makes your lungs feel like they left you, makes you feel small, and you ah . . . ah, appreciate—yep, appreciate this world a little more. I think so." He smacked his lips. He took another swig from the jug.

Bubba also claimed he had been to London and Paris and every beautiful city in this world, and he told you about each one—the buildings, the streets—and you could see it, see the names of cafes in other languages and landmarks in your mind, would swear he had been there, swear this was the truth, though everyone knew he had never stepped a foot outside of Remlap, Alabama.

I turned my eyes from the picture of the Grand Canyon, thought about Cecil's dad, the words he said when he saw that big hole. Then I walked on to Cecil's room, following the smell of his beer and the juice in his mouth.

He was taking off his shirt, hanging it on the antlers of the buck he killed two years ago. I remember cause we first started dating each other then and he was so happy about killing that deer. He's killed a ton more since but hasn't mounted a one, hasn't even kept the antlers.

"I ain't kissing you unless you take that shit out of your mouth," I said. I was already unbuttoning my shirt.

"Well, I don't want to be kissing." He grinned, spat a little into a cup near his bed.

"Then I don't want to be doing." My hands worked in reverse, putting the buttons back through their holes.

He stopped, looked at me like he did those people he was waving at on Tucker Road, and I kept thinking he was going to spit it out. My hands were over my breasts on the first button. But he waited, waited, stared at me, made me feel like I wasn't really anything, just dust off a road or a wind that you walk through, something that made the summer unnoticeable.

"Come on, Cecil," I finally said and squeezed my arms under my breasts so he could see them better, their pouting. All the chocolate in the cookie dough was making me horny.

He spat out the last of the juice, smiled and came over to me, his hands grabbing for my ass first, then working their way to where the bruise was, touching it lightly. But inside there was a kick and a sharp twist that hurt.

*

Cecil's mom might've been home by five, so I left. She knew I was seeing Cecil, but she didn't know how much I was seeing, and I didn't want her to be upset like the time when her husband, Mr. Holtin, died. When she came back from the Canyon, it was the only time I've seen her hair down, and her hair isn't pretty down. So I always keep my eye on the clock. Cecil never will.

He was out of it as usual, snoring with a pillow on his head. He'd been that way not long after he shot up all inside me, uttering something about "I was the best he ever had" and "He loved me for it." Then he fell asleep. His mamma, I knew, would find him like this, rolled out naked but covered. I did the covering to save her the embarrassment of having to see how pudgy he was getting. She always is saying to me when I'm in the store and to other people when they come in that Cecil is the weekend carrier for the post office and will be full time as soon as Bud Jones quits who is nearly seventy and should retire soon.

"That Man ain't ever going to quit," Bubba quickly sets the record straight whenever Mrs. Holtin starts up with her talk.

"Bud Jones, he's hard worker. He's been doing that route since car was invented, since we had a post office. And your boy," Bubba opens up his mouth wide as it will go, "is lazy." First time, I couldn't believe Bubba said that but he did, and it's the truth, but, boy, it made Mrs. Holtin mad. So mad, she punched the cash register two, three, four times, the bells ringing and making the roach cans shake. This was all she showed of anger to Bubba cause she thought herself polite, and, therefore, most times she tried to ignore him.

"Likes to drink all the time. That's all your boy ever does. Lazy, lazy, lazy," Bubba twisted sideways in his seat, flared his gills. "Puts the wrong mail in the wrong mailboxes anyway. What everybody says—"

"Shut up, Bubba," she yelled, her hair standing even taller, the blood rushing to it.

And I guess I should have told Bubba the same. I should have defended Cecil, too, but it was the truth what Bubba said. He winked at me then cause he got her riled up, he got her good. I tried not to smile, but I knew I did, and the two of us nodded our heads carefully.

Several times, Mrs. Holtin threatened to kick Bubba out after he said what he said about her son. But Bubba just smacked his lips, swigged his water and didn't move, stared at those cans of bug spray like he was counting all the dead painteed-on insects.

When Cecil comes in her store, Mrs. Holtin always smiles. Her whole body does a swish from her toes up, and she's extra polite.

"That colorful old man," she even says about Bubba and laughs her light flighty laugh, which is "Like Cool Whip coming out of a duck's mouth," Bubba claims. Mrs. Holtin laughs, hoping Bubba won't start talking about her boy.

One day, Cecil slapped Bubba on the back, friendly, while reaching for a can of Raid.

“Lazy, lazy,” Bubba sputtered into his jug, sucking up a big gulp and coughing.

Cecil stood there for a minute. Didn’t say a word, just stared down at the back of Bubba who was mumbling the effects of a Black Flag can— “Kills in seconds, leaves a trail for months. Kills roaches, ants, flying bugs. Sprays for twelve feet . . . .” Then Bubba started quoting the caution words.

“Let me show you some new sunglasses we got in, Honey,” Mrs. Holtin piped up and Cecil turned away, spraying the can in the air to see how far it would shoot.

“Honey!” Mrs. Holtin said, dipping below the cash register cause when Cecil sprayed, he almost got her hair.

Next time Cecil came in, Mrs. Holtin slipped Bubba three pieces of hard candy to keep him quiet, and Bubba didn’t talk about her boy.

So I cover Cecil up when I leave and take all the empty beer cans with me, crush them along with my empty half-pint and throw them in the green dumpster on my way back to town.

That day—one week ago it was—it was 4:45 p.m. when I left. I was cutting it close and at first I was jogging down the center of Tucker Road, but it didn’t take me long to feel silly about that. The Remlap city limits is only a mile from Mrs. Holtin’s house, and besides, she never takes this way home. She goes the scenic route on Rountree.

It was hot, typical July weather, and I was walking on the shoulder when a car slowed and pulled off in front of me. It was Mr. Ribbons.

He smiled, pointed to the passenger side door. I hurried in.

"Got any Chaucer with you?" I asked first thing. Since we were alone, I wanted him to know I was not afraid of knowledge.

"All my books—" He looked over his shoulder, giving the back seat a studying look. "They must be in the trunk," he said awkwardly, apologizing.

He is young. Ten years older than me, I believe, but still so young to be a teacher. His hair is straight except for a lick that curves around the back of his head. He doesn't wear glasses. He does wear long sleeve shirts. The one he had on, it was what my mother calls an ocean blue. I wonder what blue Bubba would say. Mr. Ribbons is long sleeves, straight hair, no glasses and a wedding band, and "Oh," that was all I said. I didn't know what else to make up.

His face continued with its serious look. He was studying the road, looking for something in it, something no normal person would see.

I dreamed I had sex with him one night. I was drunk and Cecil was hardly able to stand but he wanted it, said he had to have it. We were in front of his mamma's store in his truck, so I undid my pants, kicked them off of one ankle.

"Come and get it," I teased, and for some reason, I kept calling him Timothy, which is Mr. Ribbons first name—I know cause I've seen his checks—but I would never call him that, and I don't think I said Timothy too loud cause Cecil would have yelled, would have wanted to punch me if I did.

Whenever I looked up at Cecil, I saw Mr. Ribbons. He had that serious look. Bubba said he's too young to be so serious, but when I was having sex with him that serious look had me in a trance, was turning me on, and under his long sleeved shirt was hair all over his chest and arms—Cecil has just a few black hairs around each of his pudgy nipples. And while Timothy was making love to me he quoted Chaucer. He talked about months and rain and there were rhymes—it was real romantic.

I remember thinking this is what romance is. Your lover using words, saying them only to you, and lots of them, saying them seriously, with a hairy chest—Like all the people in London have cause it's cold there, is what Bubba said—while doing you.

"Is your wife out of town?" I asked Mr. Ribbons. I was studying him hard, looking for signs of that chest hair. It was thick like a pile carpet rug in my dream, and I am certain those words just slipped out of my mouth.

"No." I could tell he was surprised by my question cause his fingers grabbed at the wheel a little tense.

"Oh," I quickly said, "I heard at the store she was out of town. I was wondering if she was visiting her mamma." I said this even quicker. I could feel my face bulbing red, so I turned to watch whatever was out the window.

"No, no," he laughed, almost choking, "I don't know why you heard that." I turned back to study him.

"She's at home right now. The baby's due soon, you know?" and his shoulders eased, his fingers relaxed.

"Oh."

I wanted him. Could see the words printed on his skin under the blue sleeves, brown, brown hair. The wife taking a bath. Something romantic. I wanted to touch that.

*

Mr. Ribbons pulled into the Mustang Stop and let me out. His car zoomed on across the intersection.

I stood there watching.

Mamma would have dinner ready soon, I knew. Usually we ate some frozen packaged something that helped both of us watch our weight though she needed to watch hers more than I needed to watch mine.

She watches TV all day but turns it off when I come in so we can spend quality time together. Oprah and several others said this was important.

Mr. Ribbons wasn't coming back, as I had hoped, for something, anything, ice cream, maybe, that he needed. I went inside and Missie started talking nonstop about two guys that wanted to date her. "It's a tragic love triangle I'm in," she said. She had a habit of touching her hair while she rambled and putting on strawberry lip gloss, never satisfied with her look. So I left the Mustang Stop, walked home.

Mamma shut the TV off. First words out of her mouth were, "Our quality time, Judy." Then, "How was your day?" And, "How are you doing?"

"Mamma," I told her, "you've been watching too much TV. I'm too old for quality time." How many times do I have to have this conversation with my insane mother?

"Shhh," she put her finger to my lip, putting the *shhh*, like a candle out, her finger that smelled of cigarettes though she had told me, promised, promised on the Bible she had quit.

"We need to get along. I'm not going to be here forever, and a boulder could land on our house any minute, kill us both." She said this with her smile unflinching.

I rolled my eyes.

Her mother died when she was ten. The hospital gave her the wrong blood when Mamma's brother was born.

"Sweet Jeremy," Mamma spilled out her brother's name nicely, suddenly, as if she could read my mind. Then the other look took over her face—the memory of her mother, the blood going in and hurting, hurting until Mamma had to cry.

"You need a grip." I was serious. "Any boulder that might possibly land on us would have to come from Rock City two and a half hours away!" Everyone here lives on hills they like to call mountains. But they're just hills and nothing dangerous. I didn't fall into the trap of mentioning my uncle.

Mamma stopped crying. She has cried so much about her own mother's death that the crying can last for hours or as brief as a second or two. With her, It's hard to know which way the faucet will go.

"Dinner?" her smile returned even happier, more determined with this quality time thing.

My mother has real pretty teeth, disarming teeth.

I took the plate she offered and some sugar tea. I like mine with lemon.

I told Mamma I had a most lovely day at work, though I didn't work. And she told me what the talk shows had to say and who were their guests. Oprah was in the kitchen with somebody who had lost more weight than Oprah, and one of the doctors had on teenage girls who liked to have sex with older men.

"Too many older men." My mother nodded unapprovingly.

I ate my food.

After dinner I took a shower, since I could still smell Cecil. He's been smelling worse since his drinking has gotten worse, and I scrubbed myself harder. The streams of hot water felt like fingertips, like the ones Mr. Ribbons had on his hands—Timothy—small and soft. "I won't tell anyone," I whispered, letting his fingers touch me until the water turned cold. Then I put on some of my mamma's make-up and watched TV with her until Cecil arrived.

*

Well, it didn't take long for Cecil and me to get into a fight.

"You fucking bitch," he yelled and shoved his box of tapes into my face.

I clawed back at him, grabbing for his neck. If I could cut deep enough, maybe he would bleed to death and I'd be through with him.

"Through with your shit," I said, digging my nails in.

"Goddamn it," he shouted. He stopped the truck. He started kicking me—"Get out. Get out bitch—" kicking me, kicking.

I was able to open the door, and I wanted to scream, wanted to wake up all the people in Remlap so they could see what this bastard was doing, and all because I told him his friend Tommy Dix would be cute for Missie. I didn't say *cute* to make Cecil jealous.

Tommy Dix is cute. It's the truth. But Cecil grabbed me by the hair at the party and yanked me into his truck.

Now he was kicking me out—two shots to the chest so I could barely breathe, much less talk. He got me in the head again with his boot and I tumbled from the opening door, still grunting.

I felt like a dying roach, like I had poison in my stomach. My lungs crunched up, and his door swung wing wide. He stormed onto the pavement, his boots came closer. I tried to roll—Christ, please help me roll.

"Bitch," he spat out the word as his heels turned, and I heard my door slam, heard him walking, again, this time the other way, And I rolled like an undertow, reaching out for his boots, begging them not to leave, begging them to stay and keep me warm.

His other door slammed. The big tires squealed. The smoke smelled of burning hair. Then everything was quiet.

*

Someone poked at me.

"Young Lady. Young Lady." My back tried to straighten.

It was a reflex—I had to look proud for the police.

"Young Lady, we need to get an ambulance."

I fluttered my eyes, but the only lights were the steady overheads of Remlap—no dancing blue and red as I had imagined. I moved to one side. Damn my head hurt.

"You need an ambulance. I know you do."

"Where is it?" I asked, and my eyes fluttered, came fully open. Standing in front of me was Bubba, tugging at my shirt with one hand and holding his jug with its brown ring in the other.

"You're all bruised up, Young Lady," he sais, his jaws

clamping down heavy. "I found you," he said. "I was walking. Late as is—I'm not usually over here at this time. I don't know how, but I found you. I just did. Young Lady, you need an ambulance, someone to take you."

"Bubba," I said, "I'm fine," I assured him and wanted to stand up to prove it, but I couldn't move one of my legs.

"Stupid leg," I said. I didn't want him to worry, so I tried to wink, but the pain dug into me and soured my face. Finally, I managed to get to my elbows. I wasn't all helpless.

"You need an ambulance."

"Go on home," I told him and pushed on him, falling flat to the ground as I did, my moment of sitting up finished with.

"Young Lady, I can't leave you."

"Get the hell out of here," I shouted. I said that to this man I liked to hang around and hear talk. But before I could say I was sorry, the other sound started coming, a roar that made my head shake, then a screech that brought the burning smell back.

A door swung open, a pair of boots marched over, and I tried to roll towards Bubba, but my leg wouldn't.

The boots stopped. They were at my side, digging into me a little. Two hands came down.

"Leave her alone," a voice said. It was Bubba's.

He was pushing at Cecil's hands, arms, swatting him with the gallon jug.

"Leave her alone, Boy. She's hurt. You, you've hurt her enough."

Cecil didn't look worried—he didn't have any look. He spat on the ground and not even his belly moved much.

Then his hands cupped me under, and lifted.

"You're a Little Piece of Shit," I could hear Bubba, but he was standing back now.

"Hurt that girl. Someone should call the police." The gallon jug came flying again like a wild bird, popping off of Cecil's big head.

Cecil lowered me into the passenger seat, his heart pounding. He was sweating. And the pounding and the beer and juice in his mouth made me feel sick, like I was on a wild road, a roller coaster, and his heart was going to burst, blow up in my face and kill me.

"You're a woman beater, shit boy. Someone's going to call the police," Bubba was talking stronger now as the truck door slammed shut against my body. Cecil turned and walked towards Bubba.

As Cecil moved further away from me, the sign to his mamma's store brightened. It read—*Mrs. Holtin's Supermarket*. The letters are blue, old fashioned like a framed cross-stitching you see in everyone's home. They kind of smile down on the pavement. But it's a trick, something in the way they are written and in the light that makes them look happy.

Under the sign, I could only see Bubba's face, part of his legs—he was on the ground. I couldn't tell if it was sweat or blood hitting the pavement where he was, but he kept talking—"You lazy-bastard shit-boy. Lazy boy. Lady beater. I'm going to call the police." The more Cecil kicked Bubba, the louder Bubba got. "Lazy, piece of shit! Told everyone I could what a piece of shit you were."

I waited for the surrounding house lights to come on. But

Cecil kept kicking him, kicking him all the way to the front of his mamma's store. He kicked and kicked. And the lights didn't come on. And I didn't move. I did not move.

"Lazy," Bubba said. He could barely say it now. He was coughing between his words until the coughing was all there was.

Then Cecil's boots came toward me wet and fresh. His door creaked open, slammed shut, and we squealed off.

I looked back for Bubba. He was crunched up, still saying something—he was next to the Coke machine. It was dark where he was, and his lips moved to the overhead lights unable to reach him.

*

I wanted to call somebody, but Cecil took me to the back of one of his mamma's farms and parked the truck. We stayed there all night. All night he kept fucking me. Pumping in and out of me stronger than he ever had before. It seemed he would never stop.

And I kept thinking about Bubba, that I didn't say anything, didn't scream when he was being kicked. I didn't get out to help him. Young Lady that he had tried to help.

My leg still hurt, and as the alcohol left me, I tried to think of other things, of Timothy softly touching me, the romantic words printed on his chest. But the picture of Bubba lying there, his body pulled up like the guts in him were broken—it was too strong.

I even tried to think of the Grand Canyon, of what Bubba said about the lungs, the breath being taken and lifted, of how the Canyon was more than just a big hole. But whenever I saw this sight—imagining I was there under the bluest sky—right in that hole, right in the center of it would be Bubba's body like a silver fish taken a long time from the water, still and quiet.

Sometimes I saw Cecil's boots kicking Bubba in the sun-baked Canyon, a blur of just kick and kick. Then he would kick me and my bruises would pull, hurt, gash, and the gashes would open, groan like ghosts, like Mr. Holtin had done, grabbing his chest at the sight. One time when Cecil was kicking, I could see his mamma at the cash register punching numbers in, looking up every so often, then turning away, punching more. He left me, went over and started kicking her, pulling her hair out of her head, bobby pin by bobby pin. She didn't scream either.

By morning, Cecil had worn down, fallen asleep. I watched over him, touched my new bruises with the sweat from his stomach and arms, kept touching his hair over and over, kept thinking of Bubba, no longer the picture of him, but of what he'd said about the sky, his buddy Chaucer, how he knew everyone, had been everywhere, knew the truth in it all. When I stopped thinking of those things, it was lunch, it was hot, and I had the windows down, waving the mosquitoes off of Cecil still asleep. Whenever a mosquito did land, I would slap him into Cecil's sweaty skin. Sometimes there would be a little blood smushed up with the wings and body.

There was blood on Cecil's boots, but I didn't look there. The blood the mosquitoes drew out wasn't much. And as I waved my hands and slapped Cecil, the smell of blood and sweat in the heat became so strong, the truth of it was, I began to cry for him.

Jick's Chevrolet

—

Is a place up the hill just out of Chepultepec where the road splits two ways to home. It doesn't matter which fork you take, both go by the grass fields and the new houses being built after the March tornadoes struck. Both loop dead center into the pine thicket no one's cut down. But one day somebody will. They'll replace those trees with the bottom of the blue sky. And when that happens, you'll breathe good, so good you faint against your wheel and crash against a stump, for only so much heart pine tar and routine can be taken in at once.

But that day, my friend, is not this day. So after letting the thin card punch another ten hours off your life, get yourself to Jick's with his big blue board lit up with its pop-light sedan that trances and turns those pop-flash wheels just above the word CHEVROLET. Here you'll find all the pretty cars you've never owned—Camaros, Impalas, Corvettes, and Corvairs. Names made for riding low and pretty, made up of unreal reds and hellfire yellows, and chrome, chrome, chrome! just out of reach of your bumper and dusty windshield.

Now Jick, he's a good guy, his cars are good cars. He wants to cut you a deal. So after choosing a fork off the two-way that splits again and again like a ruthless root to divide you up, let the rubber fly. Let the maps in your head get so fuzzy you forget the way home.

Wherever you land, sleep the fuzz off till morning. Then crank your 4-banger up. Head back to Jick's cause Jick treats his customers right. He's ready to open the door to a pretty car and say, "Here you go! Give this hellfire a spin!" He's ready to toss the keys where only you can catch them. And you will, right where the sun meets your hand in the bottom of the blue sky.

Jick's cars, they crank easy, they ride fast, so take whatever cut through whatever field you have to to get to the pine thicket. On the other side, the land gets wider, emptier. And you'll fill up all that space, every last bit. Until you're as big as the sun and the moon and all the light and all the dark.

Vittate

When we danced, certain moves she made, made the bottom of her shirt lift, and I could see them—those stripes crossing her belly. And later, after making love, when she turned on the lamp to find the water glass, the stripes turned as she turned. Not tattoos but pinkish-purple scars, not deep but thin, and in rows.

"My river," she said, scratching it red at a place. When I said nothing, she told me, "I got caught in barbed wire, helping CJ put up a fence. This was before you knew us. We were pulling it tight. The wire snapped, caught me, and curled me up."

Small pinkish marks dotted her knees where lines had been and had begun to vanish.

"He should've stopped it," I said.

"That's stupid to say. Can't stop it once it starts spinning. So sudden when it does. Surprises you." She added, "Wasn't his fault."

"Awful."

"Figured you might see me that way." She went to the edge of the bed. "You always look at me like you want something perfect."

"You got me wrong. Just hate you got hurt's all I meant." I'd worked on cattle fences and knew what barbed wire could do and kept my distance. Some said the force could pick off a hand, pluck the bone from a calf if you were in front when the wire broke.

"Wire was alive," she said. "A little tornado with me in the eye, turning loud like hooves pounding. Left its mark." She scooted over, put my hands on her warm. "Goes all the way round."

"Like a striped melon."

"A what?" She pushed my body with her head then, a bull move, until we were giggling.

I'd be working watermelon fields the whole of July making decent money with my cousin, the other workers off Bucking Street, and her boyfriend, CJ, once he returned with the Florida crews. My hands ached for sandy dirt I could not shake off.

"Never tell a girl her belly is like a melon. Such a bad, bad line," she said, and I sat up, took my hands, followed her belly round her hips to her spine. Those thin ridges, how they looped a current. I wondered if the scars inside her were just as thin, if they carried the same snap of wire that hummed when it broke, wrapping her in a cruel ribbon.

"How long it take him to cut you free?" I could see his face wanting to get to her and unable.

"I was wrapped up. Thick. If I moved, other barbs stuck me worse. I was on my stomach, air knocked out of my lungs, and that pain was worst of all. Like a hammer that wouldn't let up. I don't know how long. I remember CJ's boots, the wire getting clipped, the tornado rings easing, falling back, the sun, the grass, the blood. But it was all so slow. Had that hammer on my chest. After a while I said, Don't let me die like this, cause I was afraid."

She got off the bed, which I regretted and should've apologized for—me making her tell that story, which was between her and him. But I wanted to go to the Locust Fork, the pull-in off 79, and touch its currents. If the river would let me wade to the middle where the rocks have smoothed into tongues, I'd skim my hands over all its surface.

Cheat Road

—

The story I want to tell here is one of what happens when you fall in with people. Always there's choices, but then decisions get made you can't turn from.

It was the summer Hill Pinson died. Hill was a character in this county. Worked the steel mills in B town at thirteen, then turned to gentleman farming once his bones couldn't handle the furnaces, and we saw him every weekend at the shed in Oneonta with maters, squash, the best damn okra. If you stood round his table long enough, he'd tell you a story about the county when he grew up, about sparks of steel ripping sky, about how he come to farming with no background in his family, I tell you, no background at all, but he figured things. Which he done all his life. Loud, loud voice. One of those laughs that makes you comfortable to lay in, and his cap and glasses put on in such a way you were never sure if he was looking at you or past you, into himself or out, never sure when the wheel of his brain would click a bright word onto his tongue and switch the conversation.

Stroke in the middle of a story about his neighbor's failed okra, that's what did him in—someone else's crop rotting in the earth. I kept my distance from where he held court under the shed roof after that. Whole thing put a pall on the place. In town, whatever store I went into, someone brought up Hill Pinson and his passing, so it came to be to push on a glass door was to enter a funeral parlor full of people you normally you didn't speak with. Some people go, the loss is felt wide, and maybe that was it—we had lost the man, which in turn opened up other things in me.

I've always been aware of the fields that circle people's bodies, magnetic like the one round the earth, twisting pasture-like into tall, tall grass that turns round you wherever you lay. No matter how much moving of the mouth people do, the body says this, the eyes do that, and you can be closed off to someone or open just by the gesture of a hand in that field. People have rejected me, they have given themselves to me, and it had nothing to do with what they claimed by what they told. It was their body moving tall grasses north to south without them realizing the betrayal.

When Hill Pinson died my awareness of the fields around others became more intense, and that's how I come upon it, my wife was fucking Sampson Tyler's son Bucky. My wife ain't from around here—a Texas Panhandle girl—but my family and the Tylers go way back. Sharecroppers after The War, our land butts theirs, and our bull sniffs out their two cows Belle and Annabelle. The fence between our lands we don't mend. Whatever calves get born, we split the meat.

Bucky lives in a remodeled trailer, an old Fleetwood his folks moved to a spot on their west twenty after he failed college and couldn't get a job he wanted to take. He's a young guy, and that must've been some of the appeal to my wife. He had all of time on his hands—I guess that was some of it, too. What I know for sure, when they hugged, their grasses braided so thick I was not allowed in.

I've come across two hugs in this world, the ones made with

a good slap on the back meaning respect, appreciation, but also distance, and the ones meant to sew that distance up. It's not as if Bucky had never held my wife, then suddenly started. Hell he gives me a good handshake or backslap when he sees me. We're neighbors after all. I've known him since he come into this world. But he started making sure to stand in line for Inez, my wife, at the greet and goodbye of every visit.

Didn't take long for me to catch our car at his trailer one afternoon when I cut through the woods. I got behind a cypress, sweating, listening not knowing what I'd do once I heard them. But they stayed quiet, so damn quiet, whatever was theirs was theirs wrapped up in that silver box. Shame come over me then, pushed me back to my fields, my sweat so cold in the walking, it wrung me out and the sun no help in the matter.

I could talk on about blame here. I tend to my crowders and okra too long. Hill Pinson would've had a good joke to tell about that, a man getting lost in his own garden. Inez complains I'm too hushed when we're together. "Where's your zest?" she wants to know, dropping her shoulders with the one wish to flee into the earth. In the sigh that follows, a different kind of man slips from her teeth. "All you do is draw the universe to yourself and won't let me near."

"You're the universe I'm drawing, Baby," I say it sly.

She pushes her glasses up, the ones framed with diamond fins, and stares at *Fence Jumper*, a photograph of a mule deer mid-leap over barbed wire lashed with snow. It's the only thing of my father's I've kept in the house. If I want Inez to see me, I have to move in front of Fence Jumper. I tell you, I doted on the woman, which is what my mother said to do with whoever you love.

Now I had three choices in the matter. I could kill them or one of them, though violence has never been part of my plan—I don't even own a gun for snakes. And I didn't want to carry the burden of such an act forward. I could confront Inez, but from there, what?

We'd been together seven years since her ex walked out of the cigar trees at Sun Donuts in Nectar and struck my truck window with the barrel tip of a .22. Long cigar tree pods spun and rattled while Inez pleaded with him to put the gun down. He said he still loved her. He shot the window glass to prove it, and I swung my door into his face. I come out full swing—didn't know where I was. The blood on me dropped onto him until bystanders got through the shattered echo in my ear. *Let him up!* they said. *Stop!* They lifted me. And the blood I shed was from no bullet, just shards of flown glass that had to be picked out clean. Events as such seal the deal one way or the other—either you go in with someone or you get out. I chose in, and for a time Inez was open to me. Now everything we owned was wrapped up together, and untangling a life at my age was too big to contemplate. Which left the third option—I needed someone to want.

Life is want. The whole idea of it, everything about it. To come into this world requires at the heart want, and as long as you have that, you live. Though what's desired may change for a person, I like to think I could persuade a woman close, treat her right until death does the parting. I like to think such attentiveness to a body is in me, which I have for the land like my father and his. The one you choose, she has to want the same thing though—the idea of just you two—and want it desperate. Much easier for her to travel in the mind, your body right here beside hers, resting, welcoming.

When I figured it out about Inez and Bucky I was on the Bird hard for some days, my father's give-hell-to-the-chiefs whiskey. But that rotgut gets to be its own maintenance after a while, and I can only be away from tending my crops for so long. I have to get produce to the Oneonta shed to make enough to live on my farm. I'm the last one. Give both parents to the dirt with jaws stitched, hands folded. Kept the promise I wouldn't put them in a graveyard like they feared. I have no one to hand down what they gave in their passing.

So on Friday morning, I told Inez I'd be gone till evening. She said she'd have supper ready—biscuits and tomato gravy with field peas. "Your favorite," she said, pinning a fall of hair behind her ear, but not a move she meant for me.

I took her in my arms and rocked her in that sway particular to us. She let me and smiled like we held the bond, though I knew otherwise and had to stitch that wound shut. I don't know what to tell you about that hurt except it doesn't go, someone trying to wile you into believing they still love you when they don't.

I took a small hairpin for my pocket, let her hair fan back over her face and become a river she tilted into, like what I done was a good thing she liked. Then I got to the shed and sold twenty cantelopes, six ripe red melons, all the Cherokee Purples I had. I was selling, selling the sweat to every pull-to-the-curb driver—ten half-baskets of okra and five paper bags of shelled purple hull overflowing, the butter smell of which I could not get off my hands. Kept touching the tip of my nose to smell the fresh butter. Altogether, a hundred and fifty-two in cash. Could hear Hill Pinson say, *Hell of a good take for a young man*, even though I'm not young anymore. Could feel his palm push the blade of my shoulder in. The sun had just come off its high and still none of us had put a table in Hill Pinson's spot. We let absence be the memorial. On the way home, I stopped at Lulu's.

*

Lulu is an old friend. In truth, my only one. Her life hadn't worked out well though. First son shot himself. Second run off—*Never coming back to you*, he said to her. She'd never married—*Don't want that burden* was how she put it. People left her to her grief when the first sat down and swallowed barrel. They said she was hexed and not to mess with such unless inviting trouble was your wish. Lulu had a brother and an uncle and lived by herself in a shotgun house she'd fixed up on Gaddis Williams' land. Why he let her squat, I can't say, but a lot of farmers take on a body for fifty dollars a month rent that seldom gets slapped in the palm. We all got to live somewhere, right? And maybe that was Gaddis Williams' reason. Or maybe he felt like he was doing the Lord's work. He was a Church of God man after all. I've been by that steeple and cross surrounded by parking lot cars. Never gone in. Got no use for churches or the god talked of in there since my mother forced me to hear the traveling preachers at Mercy Hill and I couldn't buck her grip. My faith is open for the taking.

I knocked on Lulu's door.

"You almost in," she called like my knock was a voice she'd

been waiting on since my last visit, which come the week after I married Inez, not sure of the ground I'd chosen for walking. I figured Lulu would calm me or kick me until I got things right. But we rowed over something, and I ain't returned to her until now. I pushed on the door. I come in, and the heat of the room pressed me back with the bloom of cornbread, for always Lulu had cornbread baking in her house.

"Inez with you?" she asked, knee-up from the floor in a cotton shirt that had pinked from its red.

"She's why I'm here," I said. I closed the door.

"But is she with you?" Lulu didn't like Inez and not just cause Inez was white. Lulu had no trust in the woman's disposition which she described as flighty, though I thought Inez had a good sense of humor about the randomness of this world having bounced and been bounced from place to place.

Lulu sat behind a coffee table. On top was a small barn she was painting on from something purple and pulpy in a jar—beautyberries she'd smashed up. She swirled them in the water, took up the brush, and took a long breath to study the tacked in splinter boards, the eaves under the tin, the tiny frames around the glassless windows, while I rocked side to side in that air of her weighing me.

"She's not with me," I said so the space between us might open. Then I made my step. I took up Lulu's hand with the brush. I lifted her.

Lulu is a tall rail black woman, one of the Pures. To have her standing next to you is to be next to a tower. Too much height for a woman, people claimed, but I wasn't afraid and I called her to me.

She held me off. "You asking me to be with you means

something more than in the past."

"I know, I take you on," I said.

"As long as we understand each other, Creek." That ain't my real name. People call me it cause a share of my blood is Creek Indian and the color shows in summer, and Creeks once lived here, though really I'm not sure I come from them. My mother never said. All my father said at the end of supper prayers was—*I got two Injuns to deal with. Help me Lord, Amen.* Some evenings he put his pancake hand to his O mouth and fluttered the woo-woo war cry. The man thought he was funny. It didn't make things better. The rest of me is a mix of white and who can tell.

Lulu is one of the Pures. Her people lived near Jade Bend where the water takes to the green of the moss rocks. They put a cypress wall around their community after the lynching of H. This was 1906. This was the old way of doing things to protect yourself and the ones you love. Guns and rumors of dynamite, enough to keep the Klan of Smoke Rise away until the schools integrated in 70, which is when the Smoke Risers walked Big Creek to burn the fortress down. Not that color tells a full story, but the Pures are said to come from one tribe on the Gambia. Even the Mexicans at Allgood Trailer Park—though they're new to here, they've already gotten mixed up with us, too.

"Creek," she said to get my attention back cause I was off thinking like I do when I'm working the fields and no one around except the silence of that god easy to get lost in.

I tilted my head to kiss her. Still she held me off.

Could smell the sharp of the berries and the high of the sun she'd been under cutting clusters, the branches bleeding out their sap milk, gumming her fingers shut. I took those fingers, rubbed them open.

"You still mine," she said. She put one hand to my face to hold the lamp of me. "Why you been gone? Hurts," she said. "Don't know if I can take you back."

"I need you now," I said. "You know my word."

"Want more than words, Creek."

"I'm bound," I said and wrapped her up and inched up her cotton shirt until all we were was skin. She let me kiss her then and carry her to the backroom. She took her grandmother's quilt, sewn of a dark blue tree branched out bright with yellow stars, to the floor. Lulu's tears, I tried to kiss them to make them stop, couldn't. Took a long time into our loving before she could, before the years between this visit and my last reached the open window.

*

So I took up with Lulu, which kept my mind off Inez. I guess I could've waited Inez and Buckey out. He'd be on to someone his own age by the persimmon frost. He would want a change by then. But the gut gets tied particular when you get old, and Inez had crossed a line from where I could not take her back. Besides, she was a drifter, had lived in a lot of *real towns* she called them—Dallas, Shreveport, St. Louis— those the ones she circled back to in her tellings. Now she had drifted from me. Lulu and I had always been stuck in Blount County. Only so many places to go, which was part of it—hell, the all of it—once you see yourself as stuck, you are.

Our summer turned into a drought that left my tomato vines a brown crisp with tiny super-ripes and less and less of them. The crowder peas and butterbeans knew how to live without much spit in the dirt, and soon that was all I had to sell. I don't have irrigation money. I live off a cistern fed from my roof gutter, almost empty. In a week, I'd be hauling a tank to the water authority, asking the man to let me fill it. Baths had to be taken in the Fork, and I come out smelling like bream. All summer I breathed like bluegills wanting to get back to their mud water.

Lulu's shotgun was on the Fork, and I went to her after selling at the shed. Some mornings the haze on the road got so chalk white, I went to her straight and gave her the peas and beans to cook for us later.

We loved on the tree branch quilt cause that's what mattered—touching skin, sweating breathless, the holding after. Then we took a cherry laurel bowl her uncle had made to the Fork and soaped up good. She dipped the water careful to separate it from the floating algae. She splashed me until I was shivering clean, and I did the same for her. Sometimes I flung the Fork in Lulu's face. She doused me good then—washing one another were the times we laughed. After, she stood dog wet, her tall lean bowing to the wind, pulling it, sieving it, not caring if I watched.

"Where I grew up is leaving me," she said one afternoon, standing knee-deep in the water's cool. "My mind's getting forgetful."

"Don't let it," I said.

"Can't help it." She looked at me sitting in her lull, in the shadow of a bank sycamore.

"I was sleeping, couldn't sleep that night the Smoke Risers showed," she said. "I still get in fits and have to come to the river, let the water cool me safe. Back then there were cries from all the houses. One house cries, you might not hear. But when everyone cries, it breaks open the night, and you know there's trouble. There was the crack of fire on wood, smoke. I'll never get that smoke out of me," she said fast.

"My uncle come in my room and pinched my shoulder with a lift while the smoke floated through the boards, hanging round the ceiling like a cloud. 'Lu!' my uncle yelled, shakiing me awake. He wrapped me in the quilt, the one I still have of the blue tree, whirled me in it, threw me over his shoulder. My uncle ran so fast I thought we flew. Whatever was the weight of me was gone. But no, he put me on my toes in the center of the others, and he held my shoulder, held me up so I wouldn't get trampled. He told me later he put us in the center, so the fire couldn't get us. 'You want to be the pit in the peach,' he said. 'The pit survives.'

"The Smoke Risers called after us, howling. They hid back in the woods where the fire's light couldn't reach. We run up Tucker Mountain to a cave that's been there even before the Creeks, my uncle said. That was the one luck—had a place to go. The ones with rifles stood at the entrance. The rest of us swatted bats. Then everyone's murmurings changed to a wail no one could hush. I breathed it in, could not push it out. I put the wail so far down in my gut, it crushed me into the damp of the cave. I remember thinking, I have nothing." Lulu said.

"That night, the water trapped in the trunks boiled until

bursting—that night of sleeping, couldn't sleep. When a morning storm took the fire, we come down the mountain. My feet, they were shoeless and sore. The smoke and fog coming off Jade Bend rose high enough to make one thing clear—nooses hung from branches like Spanish moss."

"Must have scared you to see that," I said.

Lulu shook her head. "The wailing got rid of what was in me that was scared. Those nooses made me angry cause no walls where they'd been walls, no homes where there'd been homes. I yelled for the Smoke Risers to come out of hiding, and the adults shushed me. Didn't matter. The Risers were gone and our way was over. Felt it then. Feel it now." She took my hand, wrapped it in her fist, put it to the center bone between her breasts, and the grasses round her body rolled me so deep, before I could figure myself in this new place of Lulu, I was expelled hard. I fell into the water choking.

"You all right, Creek?" she said, but her body was the one shook of what couldn't be wrung out.

Sometimes I couldn't love right because of it, my mind still in the soot and smoke trying to run clear. All I could say is, "I'm made of rust."

"You'll get it next time, Creek," she'd say and keep saying and laughing until I did. This was the other time the weight lifted, which was how the summer went after Hill Pinson passed. Me over at Lulu's, Inez at Bucky's, my bull in the Tyler's field with their grassy cows, our home—mine and Inez's—becoming a lonely place cause homes feel love or feel empty. And the summer would've gone on like that if it hadn't been for Lulu's brother. When you go in with someone, when you bound to them, you bound to their whole family, and Lulu's brother had always been trouble.

The last day of August, another Friday, I pushed on Lulu's door, pushed that cornbread back. She made love to me all stiff. After, we slung our shoulders atop her grandmother's blue quilt. In one corner of the backroom sat the buildings Lulu had tacked together, painted—her old community. Most of it was in shadow, except a row of houses facing west. The sun drew the dust from the tiny glassless windows to the big window, and the fan on her dresser swirled that dust into a milky way I put my hand through to cool. But none of my sweat cooled, and my shoulders couldn't relax.

"What?" I said.

"Sharp," she said. That's her brother. "You going to have to get him before Sheriff Pinkie Sligh gets him. Or the other boy's people. Sharp's out on Cheat Road." All of this was bad news. Sharp had killed a boy out at The Bobbie Trap. He had a thing for a white girl there and so did the white boy from B town.

"Two men wanting the same woman is never good," I said, knowing it was worse cause there was color in it.

"Go and get him," Lulu said.

"And do what with him?"

"Bring him to me."

"What you plan to do with him?"

"What I have to." Her voice kept rising.

"You can't protect him," I said.

"He's my brother. He's from the fire, too. The Smoke Risers didn't get him."

"That was a long time ago."

"Sure was, longer than us."

I sighed. "How you know he's on Cheat?"

"Stop messing. It's where he is. And you'll do this for me."

There wouldn't be any laughing and playing in the water that afternoon, so damn hot, I could've used bath.

"You bound to me," Lulu reminded, "just like I'm bound to you."

"I know," I said, "but I could get hurt."

She sighed. "Don't go fading into a coward, not today, Creek. There'll be a time when you want more from me than this." She cupped my hand to her small breast and gave that orange a squeeze. That's what she liked to call them, saying, *I got an achy orange* as warning before we got to loving when one or the other hurt. All I wanted was to laugh and feel lighter.

*

The afternoon sun hit the ridge tops white, pulsing the air with heat, no letup as the cicadas started up brave, and I took the road some call the Heart of Dixie, to Smoke Rise. Saw a truck with Confederate flags behind the cab poled to the bed corners and the cab full and the bed full of white boys twitching at blued rifles with the wind pulling at their green shirts and the crosses in those flags, trying to tear off stars. The one boy killed by Sharp—these were his people. I saw the Jefferson County plates once the truck passed my truck on a straightaway, these boys with their jaws set, their eyes crowded in purpose. Shoulder after bowed shoulder carried a particular mix of righteous anger, meaning something bad would happen if they could bring it. I knew they'd fury across the county looking for Sharp until tired of finding nothing and pretending to be wolves, they'd turn back into coyotes and tuck tail home. So I kept my steady pace. I watched the flags whip around a curve of pines before I slowed and made a U. Half a mile later, I took the hook onto Cheat.

A dirt road and unmarked, Cheat's rise and fall crosses the Yawing Swamp into the Straights, then steps up Heart Attack Bluff. There's no switchbacking when it drops out into H's field and rolls to a stand of loblolly pines that spear the earth so you can't drive into them an inch. Beyond those pines, if you walk, is where the Pures made their stand at Jade Bend. To the east is Osanippa, our tallest ridge. Below Osanippa, the Five Points where all our waters meet to make the compass and spit out the Fork.

Cheat's haunted cause of what happened to H. A black sharecropper, he was strung from a tulipwood in the center of the field for fucking a married white woman. Though some say he never slept with that woman, nothing done before the rope gets pulled matters.

After his body was cut down and took to be buried, the landowner, Pick Shell, said he couldn't breathe right when he walked his rows for his part in what happened. So he sold every acre to Tom Cheat. When one of Tom's sons shot his brother under the tulipwood, people said there it was—H's ghost had a hand in it. Tom took it hard, his favorite dead. Tom took a dive off Osanippa. The other son never yielded a day to jail, a pardon to live with what he done and lost, people still claimed. He's a Smoke Riser now, and H's field and all the wooded acres attached have been bought and sold so many times, none of us are sure who has the land. Probably a hunting club out of Florida. Those rich boys like taking what's ours.

When Lulu and I were teenagers and school was out, summer nights were about stealing whatever breaths we could from the heat. Lulu chauffeured victims down Cheat in her Merc, telling the stories of H and Tom and his sons while I hid behind the tulipwood, a rice sack over my head, a cow rope from my father's barn itching my neck in a noose.

Lulu flew down Heart Attack Bluff. She stopped dramatic in front of the field and honked her horn seven times—the number required to wake the dead. If need be, she'd tell her passengers, "Get out."

They paused before cricking open their doors, before letting the broom sedge slick their knees into the field's trough that led to the tulipwood where I was whispering for them to come closer without them hearing. Legend was if you asked H any question, he'd answer before killing you. What they asked—*Does so and so like me?* Wasted things. Or sometimes they asked, *Why does my mother hate me?* The heart of things people can only ask ghosts. Other times there were no questions. *I don't want to die*, they said even though they'd walked into the thing they had to know was coming.

Our first victims, I jumped out clawing air and yelling. By August, I stepped out from behind the tree, a slow walking shadow, refusing any answer.

They always froze up, their legs twisted. Some pissed themselves. Then they'd run off cause Lulu had locked the car and tucked herself away.

When she reappeared, walking the trough to me, she put her hands to the rice sack and pressed in. She pressed a corner of my sack-chin, flattened my ear, ruffled my hair to my head. And I took her shoulder, where it smoothed up her neck, slipped my fingers across her lips, her small bone of nose spreading skin to cheek where maybe I found the lightest tears, quivering.

Sometimes all we did was commit touch to memory. But sometimes she walked a step faster, put me to ground, and we fucked. Lulu didn't let me pull the sack off or the noose, and she lay me then like she was trying to get at something, which led to her punching my face and moaning with the strikes until *Stop*, I said. I pulled her close to ease her, but her fists kept hitting my ears with that flyby song, and knocking grass roots out of the dirt until her heart took off its hoof. She was breathless, wet-faced, knuckles bruised and cut to bleeding. I said to her, *I got you,* over and over, rocking her. Once my ears caught the scratch-roll of wind over sedge and bluestem, I took the sack and rope off. We smoked dope until we decided our victims had been scared long enough. Then we took to Cheat honking, our arms out the windows, us calling like you would for a lost dog. They crossed in front of our lights deer-eyed and got in.

I still feel those punches. Kick when they come on, pinning me deep within myself, and I have to stretch my jaw to drain the fluid of that time into my throat. Lulu's got scars on her knuckles if you look, more than come from my face or the dirt in H's field. She always fought back then, *Cause I have to,* was what she said. Despite the hard in her past, she was lucky in one way—Lulu had a connection to it. She had the miniature houses and barns tacked together. What side of my family was Indian, I knew nothing of. My mother had married into hiding and she stayed hid from me.

My family's land come from the white side and them proud of the fact. My father nailed the four corners of the Confederate flag over the window in his bedroom to let neighbors know who he was and kept himself on his bed Sundays. He wouldn't go to church with us, wouldn't step a foot out except for a bathroom run to piss out beer and Bird, as if all the sunlight through the red triangles and stars and blue cross could burn away whatever color he had in him he would never admit to. My mother bleached her face to get rid of her dark. She kept me in long sleeve shirts when I was young, especially in summers. But there was something cool about the Indian part of me in high school. Everyone claimed to be part Indian, yet I was the one to show it. Marked me different in a way the white and black boys respected and the girls took interest in. White girls especially curled their heads on my shoulder to whisper they wanted to fuck. Made me not trust white girls until Inez. For my mother was ashamed of her skin and her shame was the first thing sewn into me. The longer the days grew in summer, the darker I became—the fabric of the shirts were not thick enough to help—and the greater the distance I kept from my father. How those girls in school had approached me was lies.

I read what Andrew Jackson did to the Red Stick Creeks at Horseshoe Bend, and yet, knowing about that battle never got me any closer to my past. So I drove to where the Red Sticks were killed. Breathing in that air and shucking pieces of broken pottery out of their clay bank gave nothing over.

I drove to Tom Hendrix's wall on the Natchez Trace—this being the other time I left the county searching—his wall made of stones he took from the Tennessee River every morning after breakfast for thirty-three years before passing. He pried them from the shallows, hauled them wet and heavy to his truck, drove them home and stacked stone atop stone to dry into the steps his great-great grandmother walked when she was forced onto The Trail of Tears. Once she reached Oklahoma, she slipped back to Alabama without the soldiers knowing. *Cause she missed the Tennessee River,* Tom said, simply that. He kept her numbered steel badge for anyone who doubted.

Even seeing her badge, its silver sun in his palm burning, seeing the endless current of stones he built into a second channel of the Tennessee before he died, and listening to him tell her stories—for his mind was made clear with each word of her journey he spoke of—even with all that, my past stayed separate. Cheat Road, on the other hand, I knew, and to be on it again stretched me out good.

I followed the dirt gravel through the Straights alongside the Double Run embankment, where the tracks used to run from the Florida Panhandle to Memphis, and up Heart Attack with Big Creek way below full of muck at the neck-high spot. From there to H's field, and from there back up Heart Attack and down a second time just to be lifted into who I'd once been. The dust I made deviled up a band, trapping red and purple light.

I drove careful to see if Sharp would show himself. He knew my truck cause I'd given him rides home from The Bobbie Trap the times I was there and him too drunk to turn his own wheels. He lived above Pice's Hardware in Cleveland. Whenever I took Inez out to Swann Bridge, he'd be there with a group of mudders, tearing up the earth at the low between Swann and Scare 'em Bluff. That was his sandy ground, and he'd give me a salute.

I saw him a lot when I was with Lulu, so he knew of me, and back then, I would've told you he was a kid brother. I saw him that way. Sharp has no hair to speak of. He keeps his head bald so the scar on his top knob, where a cousin broke a branch, can shine up proud from his skin. He's a lot thicker than Lulu. Not as tall. She's the height of her family—a beautiful bone rail. He'd been a kid brother, then he wasn't. But I didn't feel regret about that. Lulu was the one counted from those days.

I turned the engine off at times to coast and listen in case Sharp was in the ditches, behind the trees. What I heard instead was the whooshing call of summer cicadas that hadn't mated. Them and the crickets vined the dark mossing over the light until a horny whippoorwill took over, insistent, as they do.

I stopped the longest at H's field. It was still here, the tulipwood. Had been for a hundred years and would for a hundred more. Would mark my death, I knew, and when people come to the spot, none would have a thought of who I'd been, but that scarred trunk and those knotted branches would hold in their center like it did mine, branches sprawled out like the roots of the earth upturned, shaking out stars, shaking out birds and all our ghosts. It was that kind of tree. I whispered across the pasture to it, then drove on to where you can't take Cheat anymore—the stand of loblollies. Parked and took my cane. My keys, I slipped down in my pocket.

It's not that I need a walking cane, but it come out of the Calvert Prong, helped me cross one May with the lilies in bloom and Inez wanting to be in the shallows where they were. Prettiest I seen Inez. Made so by that place and her love for it. She got down in the lilies not caring how soaked she made her Momma's dress of linen—Inez had all her momma's dresses to wear cause she had the woman's hips from the pictures I've seen, and she handed me her diamond fin glasses and leaned her head back to let her hair drift dark in the current over the rocks. If any place was her true home, it was that one.

The cane was hickory I had sanded and put oil to more than once to protect it. My waist high, a found cane you might call it. Could only be found by me, only fit me, and no one else. So I set the cane on the passenger side, let it rattle against the door.

Plus Sharp had killed a boy already—knifed him through the neck. He was scared. And he still had that knife.

The loblollies took me, whispering like people have told, for pines grow up to catch sound with their needles, record it in their rosined circles. They play it back when the wind pushes. Unless a storm upends them or lightning burns them or people wanting progress get out their saw. I wish I could decipher what the loblollies had to say.

A quarter mile more I was at the ruins of the Pures. Not much left except busted roofs fallen to the ground, rafters with burnt, bubbled skin, wide stone chimneys left standing with hearths waiting to be filled with kindling and fire. Wasps jittered, wrens squawked unhappy with my presence as I figured which roofs were the ones from Lulu's miniature community.

She'd set that world atop a sprinkling of red dirt she took from Gaddis Williams' field. And whenever I woke up on the quilt, I stared at the red dirt streets between the houses, figuring the routes for Lulu and me to go walking. Now I was on the very spot, and slowly, I made the compass. Lulu's house was northwest. I wanted to find her in the dog fennel running with no slow like she said she used to do until the other kids tagged her out. *My breath run the hardest then*, she told me, *cause I was frozen, trying to lay off, trying to become invisible, even to the trees.*

But everything here was too far gone. I could not find Lulu's house or her, so I slid down the sand embankment to the low at Jade Bend. There, footstep atop footstep, and a stump of wood with liquor bottles and a jar of toothbrushes, silver spoons, and forks. Next to the jar, paper napkins flitted under a hunk of limestone. Next to the stone, rolling papers and a hairbrush. All of it on a yellow paisley shirt made tablecloth. Up by the Bend was a foldup chair folded out. A blanket with a lion's face hung off the back. That chair opened to where the water made its turn under sycamore and live oak and beech.

"Sharp," I said, "where are you? It's me, Creek."

He wouldn't answer—if it was him who was here.

"I've come to get you for your sister," I said. I dug the end of my cane into the mud.

"They'll get me."

I turned and turned trying to find where his voice come from, but the water and the hanging-over branches and the mosquitoes swallowed Sharp up.

"Your sister ain't the law," I said.

"She worse," he said.

"She's your sister."

"I don't claim her, not today. Go on home, Creek. Tell Lu I'm fine but I ain't coming."

The water's surface was shadow, the sky above, shadow, but in the morning the sun would lift the lid. Jade Bend would be green translucent. The bottom of it would appear endless. A sacred spot and being in such can make a person do things they wouldn't otherwise.

I walked to the chair like I was not to be messed with and sat down to face the smooth rocks in the water.

"I promised your sister I'd bring you. That boy's people, the one you killed, they're riding around with guns. I saw them, and I ain't leaving till we go from here together."

He laughed like he was close behind, which is a trick coyotes like to play.

"You ain't coming with me," he said.

"Nowhere for you to go but with me," I said. "Pinkie Sligh's looking for you. That boy's people. Your sister, she's the only help."

"She worse," he said. "I've dealt with her before like this. You don't know."

I put the cane across my lap. "Come out when you ready." Then I put my hand to my neck and rubbed it as apology for making it vulnerable. There was a cut over the water at the center where the oak branches dipped and stopped—they could bend only so far before breaking and splashing. In the cut, a coolness sank down or maybe the cool was rising from the bed, spreading out. Either way, the shore was a reprieve from summer.

*

What woke me was not a knife in the throat, but a truck engine—mine—cranked into a steady tick followed by gears changing. By the time I stood, the halo of headlights and red tail were climbing Heart Attack Bluff with my key still in my pocket. Sharp said he would go, and he did.

The hairs on my arms pulled the sweat, left me itchy. Up top the milk of the Milky Way held the stars in a lazy band, pointing me this way, that. All I had to do was step into that high air, follow whichever path I wanted. I couldn't make the step. Instead, I turned to the bank of sycamores, their crowned leaves visible on the surface of the water in waves of flicker. I followed the rippling back to Heart Attack Bluff, the lights from my truck gone, the tick of the engine gone. Lower in the trees at the top of the sand embankment was a figure.

Jade Bend's cooling trail drew the wind down, narrowed my breathing. *Might be it for me*, I said to myself, and a new wound opened in my gut—Inez would get my family's land. She deserved something for letting go of her real towns, but what she was doing, and no children of our own to give what my parents gave—I rather Lulu have it. My wish would die here if I wasn't careful.

I tried not to think of dying, of H or Tom Cheat or his lost son up ahead in the dark. I kept my steady walk up the bank despite slipping in the sand. *Whatever is to come is to come*, I told myself. The flickering body darted out. I struck it with my cane's handle, and the body turned from running to grab at me but fell to the sand and briars instead, and there the body lay, arms glowing blue, the collarbones and calves, wherever the hem of her dress stopped. I put the cane down. "Miss," I whispered. I said it louder against the frogs.

I put my hand to her and a breath from her pressed back, thank goodness. She had the smooth skin of the young. Maybe she had a phone. All young people now have phones. But her skirt pockets were empty except for some wadded up dollars and a tube of lipstick. There was no calling for help, and I couldn't lift her. So I stayed there dabbing with my shirt at the blood coming from the back of her head. Prayed she wouldn't die. Causing her death, if I was the one to do it, made me want to do damage to myself, and I moved the goose handle of the cane close to my ear to keep it in check.

She didn't stir but her blood did stanch. The frogs and cicadas paired off, the crickets and the whippoorwill too. Only the barred owl was left to call out time while the mosquitoes worked their needles through my damp shirt. I slapped at them until morning lifted them to the shade, leaving me alone to make her out. The light was still a dark light, yet I could tell she was one of the fake whites with fake blonde hair, which made her even whiter like when my mother bleached her skin. The blood the only thing on her sticky and dark.

"Girl," I said and shook her gentle—she had to be the one from The Bobbie Trap the fight was over— "Girl," until slowly she roused.

She looked at me startled, got ready to yell. I held her shoulders down. "Mean you no harm," I said what I knew she wouldn't trust.

Her yell went up through the branches, which caused the ache in her head to rise. She grabbed at the knot in back and dropped to the ground crying.

"What did you do?" she said.

"Didn't know—"

"Why?"

"If you meant me harm," I said. Though there was no excuse

striking someone running away.

"Sharp left me here, Creek," she said. She knew who I was, and as her short breaths filled her figure, I knew her—Belle Gin. Her mother handled books for Oneonta Lumber. Her father had worked coal in Walker before dust silted his lungs and insurance had to provide a nurse to take his care. I knew Belle as a girl up at the market. I sold her family purple hull and white acre, and I've seen her work the moon stage at The Trap. First time it was difficult to separate the two—the girl, the young woman. But people grow up, at least their bodies, and there cannot be shame in that. The row between Sharp and the boy from Jefferson had been about Belle Gin and I pulled away.

"Don't look at me like I'm dirt. Sharp left me here—you and him's dirt."

Every one of my protests got punched down my throat, so I changed thoughts, managed to ask if she had a car.

She laughed. "I can get rides." The sun's first bands were coming over Osanippa then and the pain come on her and she winced, but she was able to pull herself up to sitting while the bottom curve of the sun pulsed the leaves. "Could've left the county clean yesterday if we had had a car. Sharp wanted to hide out 'Where no one will find us,' he promised. Then you show up." She shook her head and this hurt too. "No man has ever made a good promise to me, you know that? What's wrong with you, Creek?"

"Sharp the one left you here," I said.

"Better that than getting struck by an old man's cane."

I started to say something about not being old. My cane was lying on the ground.

She swatted a yellow fly, brushed it off. "Thought I was dreaming when I heard your truck in the middle of the night."

"I thought so, too," I said and mapped the roads out of the county, saw Sharp on all of them frantic and figuring. Maybe he wasn't on any map any longer. If Pinkie Sligh had stopped him or the boys from Jefferson. Or he could just be gone.

"When I heard you coming up the bank, I should of run right then."

"Sorry," I said. I didn't like that sound in my mouth, for sorry is a coward's word. I said, "We can try to get to the Heart of Dixie before it gets hot. If you can walk with your head sore."

"I can take care of myself here. Got food and water. You go on."

"I could use a drink. Food would be a good thing."

"You go on," she said. When I said nothing else, she sighed. "How does it look?" She tilted her head.

The puncture in the knot had swollen shut, none too bad considering the force I put in when I struck her. I almost made a joke about her being hardheaded, but to look at the swell and the blood dried in her white hair—there was disappointment and anger at myself for what I did. I held my hands out like they were not a part of me, like they had done the damage and I should scold them, though scolding part of you is a ridiculous thing—all of me was to blame.

"I'll clean it so you won't get an infection," I offered and we kept quiet.

Sometimes it's not that people come to a clear understanding, but between Belle Gin and me was enough of one.

*

I soaped her wound with a yellow bar, poured water over the cut until the dark crust washed out of her hair. I ate thin bread slices—all she had. She took off the brown crust and rolled what was left into dough balls. We drank water from plastic bottles they'd carried in. Then I spent the day under a pine branch in the lion chair staring at Jade Bend as it purled over the rocks. I took measure to the limestone bottom while she rested on a sleeping bag to soothe her ache.

Lulu had played here, had splashed in the riffles like she splashes me in the afternoons at the Fork. When she comes out shivering, I take her to the quilt, and the blue tree and yellow stars soak up our wet as we laze on top of the floor. Sometimes, I dream of weather turning so cold, Lulu has to put the quilt back on the tick, the edges tucked in so tight, she has to unlock one corner, me the other until we're rolling underneath the branches warm.

I thought of Inez, too. I knew she was sitting on our sofa staring at the photograph of Fence Jumper, putting extra pins in her hair to pull the roots. She was waiting for the deer to touch ground, which is what she does when she worries. I hadn't come home, and she doesn't sleep well without my body next to hers. Despite everything, we still had our routines and I was out of mine.

Then I thought of Hill Pinson, his story about working Sloss at nights, iron flecking up from the furnaces.

Some sparks, he said, *flew all the way to the Highway 1 Bridge*. The furnaces were under that bridge and he raised his hand to show what long distance the sparks had to travel.

He said, *Lovers used to pull over to the shoulder, hoping those red stars would reach them so they could make a wish upon.*

Hill Pinson said he didn't have time to be a lover—work was his lot. He said, all the stars eventually fell, and when they did, *They pelted our suits. They pinged to the floor*. And Hill Pinson stood with the other men afraid to move. *It was a kind of rain*, he said while looking to where the iron had been and still was to him.

"Creek, come over here Creek," Hill Pinson called from somewhere down in the limestone bed. The shadow of his hand pulled at his cap, gesturing in the current, but he was not here. This is what happens when the tall grasses round you turn inward—they unthread you—and in that wide space, your ghosts come to drink.

I pushed myself up in the chair, was about to walk out into the current to cool off my sweat and clear away my dreaming-self, when my truck's engine ticked over Heart Attack to the loblollies and stopped.

Sharp knew this place better than I did and best to face him here in the open, so I pressed down on the cane. I kept an eye on Belle Gin. Wasn't long, he called for her from the rtreeline.

Belle Gin got up stretching, turning her body into her dress's corners. "Why you leave me here, Sharp?" she said.

"To get money so we can get out. No one's going to expect us in Creek's truck."

"Pinkie Sligh's got roadblocks," I said.

"I can get around them. Already been getting around."

"I told you we could've left the county clean yesterday," she said.

"Shut up," he said and his echo skirted across the water.

"He hit me." Belle Gin pointed to where I was. "That old man knocked me out with his cane. You shouldn't of left me here."

I edged to the waterline, to where the sycamores curled their leaves to catch the sunlight, wondering if they would catch me, too.

"I told her I was sorry. Didn't know who she was. It was dark." And I looked for him to come charging like a bull. I looked and looked for his baldhead full of sweat.

"I got no problem with you," was all he said.

"So you going to let him?"

"I'm ready, Belle Gin. Come on."

She handed me a stinging look before starting up the embankment, sledding speckled sand aside, and I geared up to make my own bull run, to find Sharp, to knock him some sense.

"Saw my sister," he called out. "Lu gave a message."

I leaned on the goose handle.

"She said, 'Tell Creek he's not bound to me anymore.' Said to make sure I told you that."

I could not separate the field around her body from mine, so I didn't answer. I didn't move.

Belle Gin walked into the ruins. Wasn't long, my truck engine started to tick, and what took me next was something dark—Lulu's brother had hurt her, maybe killed her. That's why he said that she said that. Only this made sense. Unlike the other thoughts that had churned slow out of Jade Bend, the thought of something happening to Lulu triggered a quickness in me.

I climbed the sand embankment, run past the wasps and wrens and fallen roofs and chimneys of mortared stone, but when I stepped into the loblollies, gunshots come over and I halted. The echo started the needles to whisper until the whispering got so loud, it bled out an argument between me and Lulu like a radio tuned high. It was the argument from all those years ago, the one that had set time between us then just as time was set between us now.

Lulu yelled, "You married *her*. So you must not want me."

I said, "Don't be a nigger."

Lulu busted out laughing. "What, like you?"

My father had told me his whole life, *At least you're not a nigger*—my worth to him as a son. How often my father put that word into me.

"I'm not," I said cause my father said.

Lulu leaned over the oven to cut two slices of cornbread out of her mother's skillet. She got butter from the fridge. She put it on her slice and the second slice. She dropped the second into my hands.

"Ow," I said. I had to shift the slice around. She had pulled the skillet out of the oven just before our argument, so we couldn't have been yelling long for the bread to be so hot.

She took a bite. "Everyone is. Most people just afraid to admit it. Afraid to know themselves is all."

She kept blowing on her cornbread to cool it, then taking a nibble. I held on to mine. I let the steam push my palm red.

"I'm not," I said.

"Don't be afraid, Creek."

*

I come out of the stand with the cane lifted, ready. Up ahead was my truck, exhaust pouring out the pipe. Just beyond facing it was the truck with the Confederate flags, the wind whipping those colors open.

Both my doors were slung wing-wide. No one in the cab. No Jefferson boys in the other cab. Through the dead grass was a path, and I walked the trough. Two bodies were ahead, bleeding out into the bluestem. I knew the white hair, the other body's proud skull, but I did not go where they lay.

Instead, I looked around for H to come out from behind the tulipwood. Surely, it was his ghost that had brought this on—he'd be looking for me now. Only, I was the one who had played his ghost to scare friends in high school, and I felt the rope squeeze tight round my neck. Not a real rope. The one from the past I had put there willingly. I stared out at the square of the field, the tulipwood in the center. I stared so hard, the twitching leaves blurred and I could not see a thing. There was plenty of time to see things right if I could slow my heart down, figure where I was.

"Lulu," I called for her like I did when we were resting quiet and our skin touching grass to dirt, and everyone else running to the pockets in the woods for us to catch later. Our love was made. The wind took off with her name.

Brothers

1.

Crow

—

Some evenings I get the sky I want and think of riding clouds instead of laughing coyotes. But once the sun turns blue, it gets too cold, and I have to turn in. What I want to know, brother, is how you free yourself when you're attached to a part of the sky you can't follow? I can't say I understand all you want me to, but I do feel the things you tell me. How I'm the crazy for wanting to follow Alabama clouds through winter. "The dirt is for walking," you say. "Is where we'll always be. We ain't birds." But what we can't touch, we grab hold of. Those clouds slipping across the sky, they get to leave this tired world.

2.
The Wine Boys

—

Listen. All we got is wine to drink after work and our women to love us after. So in the morning, we wake up sleepy-eyed in other people's houses, we can slip down their stairs and look for bottles in their cabinets to open at the next gathering where you and I will be so full of life we cannot be stopped. If ever we stop, brother, the silence will fill us with dirt like the kind when we worked ourselves poor for money and women refused our love. Remember that? I need to hear a guitar player playing, a saxophone-horn blower blowing brass spit to haunt up the chairs so we can sit and yell, "Got this world!" tapping our feet on wood cloud river, laughing. I tell you, that music'll follow into the hereafter. Until then, we got other people's wine to drink, we got women to love. Every night exhaustion is all we are.

3.

Whirling

—

You talk about it all the time, how your mind whirls like a thrashing machine you have to make quit. I don't want that brother. When she told me, "Lay down, don't move," I got in the grass under the black sky, set her hand to my throat, and let her check me for a fever to take to her hips and open. You claim fucking ain't real love, but that's where I'm free. I'm sure I got it all wrong. I'm sure you'll set me right. But when she started to sway what she promised, I couldn't breathe until she sent me aching up through the branches. I fell to the wet grass. I hummed finger to toe awed while she caught breath the way lazy toads catch flies, splitting starlight with her tongue. I kept wondering, if you found a dirt road for leaving on, would you.

Last time Bo Played the Blues

—

He had four fingers on his left hand. He was born that way people claim, but tonight he's got six. Now I know I've been drinking. Hell, we all have. And I know drinking is an epidemic among us out-of-work jobbers, but six fingers—Damn, Bo. We're losing money and ground to the Man while you're gaining digits. Let me say here, I can count to a high number even in a drunken stupor, so I know how to count to six. And let me say, too, the blues have never sounded this good. Amen.

Last time Bo was here, he jowled down—twisting his neck like a duck over the wavy part of his guitar, his eyes using some red laser telepathy to tell his fingers what to do. He did not. He did not, I repeat, take a break from making his guitar twang-diddy-twang. He just shifted up the fret board, latticing a ladder to the sky. He made clouds we couldn't see dance suggestive with the moon, and that was with four fingers. With the extra two, it's like he's taking us to one of those galaxies getting started. He's the usher man.

Last time I heard Bo play the blues, I was still in love with Lucinda, one of those bad loves where your woman yells at you and you yell at her and the drinking the only thing makes it good enough to stay inside that squeaky-squawking birdcage you've built around yourselves. I had just been let go from my one-week stint at the chicken plant because I supposedly cut chickens the wrong way.

Boss said I didn't know the difference between a thighbone and a backbone. Hell if I don't. I was cutting them more efficient, Fool. Calling him a fool is what did me in.

I went home glum, got Lucinda, and come out here to The Bobbie Trap. Now, did I get a single *I'm-sorry-baby* from her? No. Instead, Lucinda told me she'd fallen out of the love orbit we spent so many months spinning. All the while she fanned the yellow ruffles at the top of her blouse.

"Man's got four fingers to strum with. That's all, Ronnie." She pointed to the stage. "Yet he's got more soul and love in his damaged right hand than you'll ever have in all your life."

I explained to her that Bo was a left-handed strummer.

"Don't matter, Know-It-All," she yelled. She whumped my head. "Damn, Know-It-All, you see? You hear me? You'll never love me like he loves his guitar." And Bo was going into some deep delta blue under the big muddy cause he's from there, born out of that river. I could not breathe above the chords he kept laying down so heavy, and I had to shut my eyes. I nodded.

"You're right," I said to Lucinda. "I don't love you." She chucked a Fuzzy Navel in my face that made me taste all peachy.

"Idiot, you're not even willing to fight for our love."

But I would not open my sticky eyelashes to any of her venom. I was down underneath the river at its deepest point in the coolest channel where Bo come from. My river of peach and awful feeling feeling so good, so lonely, yet so automatic, I wasn't ever leaving if I could help it.

Her chair scraped across the floor like a fat chicken unable to fly.

"Wait Lucinda," I said in a breath of regret, but she kept on until all I had was the emptiness of where she'd once been. Up on stage, Bo continued to play the blues. He never even looked at his audience while he did, just stared at his fingers. So I looked at mine all rough cut. I wondered for a split second what kind of pieces a chicken with a boning knife might cut out of me. Then I refocused, thought of Bo's music and my fingers. Together. This was the first time I really communicated with him, on his level, when I understood where the calm in him, his eye of the tornado, come from.

I looked off, way off. Can't tell you exactly where—somewhere into the mob of tomato farmers and dirt bikers getting rowdier, knocking their wooden blocks on tables, the colored lights on the moon stage weeping above us. I don't know where it was I looked, but I connected with something larger than the world of the bar. Every now and then, I yelled, "I'm with you, Brother," and put a hand to the ceilinged sky, grabbing hold the ladder Bo had made for us to climb. Though he never answered me, he heard me. Amen.

After Lucinda's declaration on his soulful playing, you'd think she'd be here tonight at the kickoff of his tri-county tour, the place where it all started people claim. I was prepared, ready to ignore her cutoff-jeaned ass. But let the record show she is not here to witness the miracle of Bo's additional two fingers bestowed upon him by the alien god. He did not just sprout them up there on stage—I can attest—and he's using his new fingers like they've been on him his whole life, helping to take us up to some far off galaxy we never want to come back to Alabama for. Who wants to come back to taxes? and to foolish bosses? and a disco ballroom full of blitzed tomato farmers throwing their Beefsteaks at the helmetless bikers who ain't going to take it much longer, I promise? Who wants to come back to irresolute women that don't love you? Not me. I would only return for true love, if some woman could give it, and give it to me the right way with an understanding that even if I can't play the blues like Bo, I know what he feels. If I had to, I'd find a way to grow fingers just to love a true love back. Every chord he touches strikes ever so deep in me.

Ferris Wheel

—

When I come upon it, half-buried in Old Brown's field like a huge roulette wheel laid out flat and ready to be played, numbers rusted on the side of two-seater cars, 43 and 37, like psi numbers on the largest tires you've seen, though this was a heavy steel frame, nothing rubber, more like an alien vessel or a giant turtle shell with much of the bone eaten up—when I come upon it, I cogitated a lot of things *this* was like, but in truth, it was a ferris wheel.

We'd had so much rain for months I hadn't had a chance to harrow, much less plant rows for my uncle. This field, about six acres of dog fennel and briar touching on the Calvert Prong, had flooded out, and I thought the waters might of showed some arrowheads with all the muck. For years I've been walking Old Brown's land, stealing his arrowheads and selling them to Tugbail in town.

But when I come upon it, I had two visions, for I'm a man prone to visions. The first was of the ferris wheel coming loose from its cradle in the great tornado that swept out of Mississippi in March. Winds whipping so strong, they kept the contraption on its rims arolling until plop, the wheel sunk down to the riverbed and the current hurried it to this bend where the waters slowed enough for the wheel to wobble out into the silt.

The second was that this field had been the home to a great fair once, that workmen had put a midway up in lights with woozy organ music and a howling train ride. Instead of stinking mud, cotton candy and powdered sugar had been carried on the very winds that had carved the river. That, back when our town had bustled, this was the destination people rode out to to forget the hard in their lives. I've always wanted to take Oneida on a ferris wheel ride up tall as Big Tree and kiss her at the very top. She tastes like julep all summer long and would not have told me no. After winning her a prize from shooting green metal ducks, we would've taken a ride on the Calvert Prong among the floating paper lanterns and lilies. Yes, I would've have taken her down that tunnel of love if we'd lived in that time.

Maybe the fair got caught in some great flood, or maybe after a night of shine and train singing, the cock crowed everyone to work so early they forgot about this place of having fun. So the briar grew over the fair. If true, somewhere near my boots was the buried, busted out heads of horses of a carousel still going round, biting at mole grubs biting at roots.

I gave the rusty earth a kick, for that was the past. There was only one vision for the future—my uncle's backhoe. I would get it over here in the dead of night, dig the old steel up going round and round. Old Brown, he'd be dead asleep and unable to figure a thing while I worked a pulley system through the springy cottonwoods along the bank. I'd lift the wheel until upright in the branches, then I would take a sledgehammer to the giant rims and whack the muck into powdered air.

My uncle's voice would whirl in me then—*Give it a turn*—and I'd push, rock on one of the back cars until the contraption got enough grease to go. Not towards the Calvert, which might gurgle the whole thing back up. I'd go the other way atop Middle Mountain. I'd have to be strong like Atlas strong to get it there, and I would.

From that iron ore hill, you can see my uncle's land where I've planted his yellow corn and rattlesnake peas ever since my parents died and he told me how. You can see our town where Tugbail has his trading shop, where I bring arrowheads. You can see Oneida where she sweeps the porch of her mother's house clean every day, drinking her juleps, waiting for something to happen that is good. Then I'd have to choose who to ride the wheel with. Or maybe, once I got buckled into one of the numbered cars tight, I'd get so busy whirling between earth and sky, I'd forget how to brake, forget where I come from at all.

Tulipwood

—

Pick Shell, 1910

When I turned the rope round that man's neck, his skin pumped tight with blood. Now I cannot step a row without my hands burning on pink cotton blooms. It's been a year since his body was cut down, but that tulipwood in the middle of the field still bends its limb, daring me to walk under. A colored man had raped a white woman on my property, so you tell me—no matter what Arnett Gibbons claims now—was it wrong to kill a nigger for what another done? Something in their skin breeds violence. Is it wrong to expect forgiveness? When the forgiveness doesn't come, the twine in the bark takes over, stops me from living. My wife says, "Let it go, Pick. Get on with living." And for the other men who helped, this field is just a quiet place for riding past. But the wind pushes me towards the middle and the tree. The cotton pitches its blooms and the brown-white pods break rough like rope curled into palms. What I touch causes burning until I cannot walk any further. Cannot enter my own land.

*

Arnett Gibbons

They hung him for what I said, and I have to look at the road empty now of where a man had walked to his fields and worked and he isn't and can't no more. All I told, he was black who raped me. All I did was not deny what my husband, Juke, said. I never offered a name. Not to Mr. Shell who owns our farm, not to my husband who showed up after Randall left. Juke told me he had watched us, had seen what Randall and I had done, and later Juke come back with the community men from Smoke Rise. I told them he was a colored and tall, unnamed and unwanted. If I didn't my husband would've broken my face with an iron. His wife making love to a colored man he knew. What would you of done? I didn't know they'd find H Thompson walking over a mile from me but close enough, they said. I didn't know until Juke returned home, smelling of smoke and sweat borrowed from someone else's skin. "We killed him," he said. "Your man's gone now." Before he said the name, I was afraid they had found you, Randall, had figured out the turn of your steps. "We killed H," Juke said. "We've his farm to work now." Where's Randall? I almost asked, but I had sent you away. I almost cried except Juke kept staring to see if I still loved you, if I would.

*

Randall Briggs

When Arnett told me Juke had figured it, had seen me slip out of their house when I should've been in my fields, when she said the Smoke Risers were hunting me, I left as she wanted and asked her to come with, but she wouldn't. So goodbye to this damn county, every fencerow and tree. I was raised here. Goodbye to my fields—cotton soon past bloom, corn already browning. My house had been my parents' house, what they made after the war—lost, from my hands. Twice in the evening I saw men and their kerosene torches. Twice I slipped off the road. In the woods, I found the tracks to Double Run, walked quick, looking for a train. I heard the men in loon calls and crickets get closer. So I don't know why I turned round, marched for my home like I was invisible, invincible, until I came upon a man near the tracks, ankle blood-wrapped, sweating, telling of a lynching that should've been me. "Over in the field," the man pointed. "Be careful. They might want more than one of us." So I did and waited and went to the field, empty of people except for H under the tulip branch. The smoke from his burnt hair fell to my hands. H was my friend. He worked the south plot of Mr. Shell's next to mine. Now his body pulled a rope through the center of the sky, waiting for someone to cut the sky loose, so he might pass. I said, "You should've been me." But how do you get forgiveness from the dead? I couldn't lift myself or peel my body into his skin. I had no knife to cut him down. Yet he was me, and I him, his lungs and mine breathing and not. I walked back to where a train would come. The hurt man I had seen, that prophet, had disappeared. The crickets begged for each other, and the night through those pines was more than the moon could clear. What I touched and knew, I wanted to forget.

*

Train Man

I rode trains to keep myself from being stuck in one place and hitched a feed car on the Double Run just to see my aunt. Once I got close, I jumped into the woods. The sweet grain dust had made me crazy, so I was happy to spring clear. But I cut my ankle on a rock, the first of bad luck, then the second, that field where I heard people yelling.

I crawled up to the plowed edge, saw those white heads lit up with torches and I stayed hid, sneaking back further into the pines. I knew when I first tasted the rotten smoke, they had a man up there black like me. They roped him to a tulipwood, pulled him tight. Those trees are pretty in spring with white-orange flower cups you can drink out of if you pinch them from a branch. But no blooms in August. And no water. The man looked out at those torches and passed into a ghost. Torches can't burn a ghost. From where I sat, wrapping my ankle in a shirt, shaking, sweating, trying not to breathe hard, I'd never been so grateful for the darkness, his and mine together, so I wouldn't be found.

*

Smoke Risers

We went to Pick Shell's field cause the crime had happened on his land, and we poured into the acres like the cotton rows were pews of a church. In the center, the man who raped Juke's wife. We found him. We took him here—H was his name, filthy as the dirt eating at the heels of our boots. The rope whipped over the sunken branch, and someone sang out, "Hang him." We knotted the rope thick to hold his neck. Someone called him "Animal. A possum stuck in a tree." I swear he didn't look human anymore. Then we raised him and he swayed. "Kill him," we said. It sounded like "Amen, Amen." After clinching his teeth, he wasn't listening, he was floating over us all, and I knew, I knew, he would never come down and we would never go up.

*

H

They hung me like they planned to. What could I say to stop them—innocent? They'd lost that word and wouldn't hear it from me. Maybe the blood in my body, which was the same as theirs, maybe the blood, getting tight in my neck, if enough of it spilled into their lungs and forced them to cough in their singing of "Rapist" and "Hang," in their wish for me dead, maybe that's what I could do—choke them out. It's what I wished for until the burning in my throat spread. I woke up as they cut me down. I watched my body fall and heard the thud of my shoulders, my knees as if it had happened after it happened. Then boots came over my back pressing, but I was past feeling, past the torches, trapped in the moss-moon bark wondering how to get back inside my crushed skin. I tried to slip into my own gashes, into my ears, into my mouth. With my hands, I tried to uproot their boots, push their shoulders away. Still they pushed through me, for their feet and hands were real with purpose. Nothing of me was real any longer. They lifted me up. Hung me twice. No way I could unswing my body from the branch. I didn't know Arnett Gibbons that well. I knew her husband Juke better. We both rented from the same store, worked our fields to the same fence line. He stood with those faces determined, accusing and yelling, until he and them got tired of their own voices. When they walked off, I curled their faces inside my palms, told them to run on, to get. I sent them home, but what did they feel? Later, when some came back to gawk, to make sure I was dead—each bone, each muscle, each eye—I yelled at them to cut me down. They pretended not to hear, so I slipped into their skin and looked at my body through their eyes until they saw what I saw, and they couldn't take watching me pull on the limb intent on breaking break free.

.

The Story of Rountree

—

Forget the shot I took, the one to the head, that I gave myself. Remember us sitting in the back of the truck, talking about pine straw, how easy it would be to make a living gathering it, bundling it, selling it by the tractor-trailer load. People want it for their yards. Keeps their weeds out. Keeps their wet ground wet. So many pine trees here. Miles and miles of it, man. There's money in straw, I told you.

I tell you, if you'll listen, I can't remember the last time I did something that was good that didn't require fire. Every time I started a fire in a field, she showed up. Fire was what called her in, my second wife. Fire drew me close and dizzy and I fell and kissed the coals. She pushed me out from that danger. Shook the flames off me, made them into ashen stars no one can see now except on the darkest nights when the winter and wind allows it.

But that was before the stillness and the rain and I took my shot. She was putting out someone else's fire by then. She did it straight—leaving me.

Remember us sitting on the back of the truck and the melon picking done, and us heading home, hands muddy, sweaty, feeling the grit the truck's wind blew at us, and I told you about pine straw, there was money there, that that one thing was a way to see the world clear and good.

Remember, we were joking. Remember, I offered you a beer.

And you said it would be a good way, like this would not be the last time we worked a field, the last time we talked about the money in pine straw, the last time I would tell you, I loved my second wife.

Jack Who Loves to Paint

—

No one paints around here—that's the first thing I'll tell you. You have to understand, no one paints anymore except children in elementary schools, children at home with their mothers—only children. By high school, a few kids are still doing it. My best friend Tommy was one of them when we were seniors—cartoon and comic book figures, especially Conan, were his specialty. He works with me at the Truss Company now, but he hasn't done any cartoon figures since we graduated.

No one paints. Except for houses. But no one paints, paints for art. People farm or work the coal mines or the steel press shops. Some have grocery stores and gas stations to tend to. A few of us are here at the Truss Company. But no one paints except for Jack, who's younger than Tommy and me by a couple years.

You can find him in a field, one of the ones his father, who owns the co-op, has bought. Jack paints on huge canvases or paper bags. He has an easel and lots of tubes.

If you're riding by during lunch, going down the dirt road by the Church at Mercy Hill, you'll find Jack almost always painting. If he's not, he's watching a canvas, drinking sips of water from a bottle, making sure every detail is right. It can be 100 degrees or 50 degrees. Sometimes even when it's raining, lightning. He stands, too. Never sits down, which my back couldn't take.

One day I saw him throw a line of fire using his hand. It was a reddish-orange, but the way he threw the paint on with his hand was like fire. It really was.

I told Tommy who was next to me in the truck at the time that Jack was making tall flames, and Tommy nodded yes, he was, that that was exactly what Jack was doing, throwing fire.

Starting Monday, Jack moved his canvases, his easel, his paints, brushes and bottles of water to the field behind the American Truss Company.

Mr. Dawson, my boss, owns the company. It's on a quarter-acre. Jack's father, Mr. Pardee, owns the field. He sold that quarter to Mr. Dawson so Mr. Dawson could build the American Truss Company, but the rest of the field is Mr. Pardee's. And so if Jack wants, he can be here, and he has been since Monday.

Yesterday, Tuesday, Mr. Dawson called Mr. Pardee on the dialup in his air-cooled office.

"Your son is disturbing my workers," he said.

I didn't hear what Mr. Pardee said, but Mr. Dawson didn't like it.

"I don't care if it is your land," Mr. Dawson said and slammed the receiver down. But Mr. Dawson didn't have a choice—it is Mr. Pardee's land.

So today makes the third day Jack has been here. He is working on a canvas—a big one, though not too big—and he's using oils. Tommy told me this yesterday.

"What kind of paint is that?" I asked while we were nailing on some trusses.

"Oils," Tommy said.

"It looks blobby when he puts it on the plate."

"Oils," Tommy said.

"Oils, huh?" I said.

Jack's back is to us, so all we can really see are his shoulders, his arms, his legs, the heels of his feet—he doesn't wear shoes. You can also see his hair—black hair cut short and straight like he's a businessman, like he works at the co-op with his father.

It's June, it's been hot, but Jack's wearing long sleeve shirts and jeans. He wears a different long sleeve shirt every day. Monday it was yellow. Tuesday, red. Today, blue. And it looks like the sky does. Real and brilliant.

Tommy and I are wearing T-shirts. In the afternoons, our T-shirts smell like sawdust and sweat. So do our jeans.

Jack's jeans are faded and old. He always wears the same pair. The jeans are dirty. I remember them from the times I've driven down the dirt road by the Church at Mercy Hill.

I always drive slow, so I can watch him paint. Sometimes he paints calmly, sometimes like a wild man. That day he put fire on the canvas, he was wild.

Yesterday he was wild, too. Must of brushed over the canvas eight or nine times. Early in the morning the canvas was a bright pink, but by noon it was banana yellow. It looked like a banana—a square canvas banana. There were several other changes, more colors he added. And, by the time we left work, the canvas was a deep crimson red like the Alabama football team. When I drove by later that night about 8:30, the sun was starting to set and he was still there. Jack was still painting. The canvas was almost completely black.

I wanted to go up to him, ask him when did he go home, but

I didn't.

All morning today, Wednesday, the painting has been a magenta color—Tommy told me this was what you called that color. Not purple. Not red. But magenta. Magenta.

"Y'all stop staring at that damn boy painting," Mr. Dawson says to us. It's the third time this morning he's said it. "The order has to be filled by 4. We have to be in Snead by 5." The city of Snead is thirty minutes up 75.

I keep my head down low and hammer at boards. I hammer faster and faster until Mr. Dawson goes in his office. His office has the windows open and the box fan to air cool it, and a TV set. The TV is always on. You can see commercials, game shows, and soap operas coming on, but you cannot hear the conversations or applause. The volume he keeps off cause Mr. Dawson is always on the dialup with a customer or his wife. Usually it's his wife. Their house is next to the Truss Company and she is almost always there. She brings Mr. Dawson lunch every day. Sometimes she brings us lunch. She jokes that she lives at the house and Mr. Dawson lives at the Truss Company.

"You won't ever come home," she teases him with a pointed finger, so they stay on the phone a lot.

Mr. Dawson opens the door to his office and comes out. I start hammering faster.

"No lunchbreak today," he makes the announcement we knew was coming. "That order," he says. "4pm. Snead, by 5," he says. "I'm going to have Charlene bring over something to nibble on."

Charlene is his wife.

"Is she going to bring some of those biscuits?" Tommy asks.

"I don't know," Mr. Dawson says. He rubs his chin.

Tommy lowers his head, pushes another board through the saw. The saw screams. Then the board is cut and the screaming's over.

Mr. Dawson returns to his office. I'm still hammering fast. Mr. Dawson is picking up the phone.

"Did he pick up the phone?" Tommy asks. He's trying to whisper, but the saw is so loud, he can't.

I nod that he did.

We both know Mr. Dawson is calling Charlene, and we'll have biscuits.

I slow down on my hammering and look at Jack. His face is still turned away from us. He's in the middle of the field, painting.

The Truss Company is off Marshal Farms' Road. Behind it is the field. Behind the field are some woods. They go up a ridge—pines, oaks, hickory, cedar—like that. Jack is in the middle of the field, facing the woods. Beyond those woods is where the sun comes to set.

He's not painting fast today. He is painting very slow.

On the right hand side of the painting, the magenta is starting to turn redder. He keeps stroking in red lines, then picking up a sponge and scrubbing over the red until it blends in with the magenta as if he's cleaning the painting. The magenta becomes lighter after each scrub.

Jack stops to drink from one of his water bottles. He has been stopping more to drink cause it's 11:30, and it is hot today. The tin roof over the truss company is popping from the heat. It sounds like chicken necks being wrung.

Yesterday was Tuesday. It was 103 degrees. Today is supposed to be just as hot.

"Stop watching that damn boy painting," Mr. Dawson says when he comes out of his office. I hammer at the boards in front of me faster and faster, beating dents in the wood. I keep my head low.

*

At 12:30 Charlene gets in her car and drives over to the Truss Company. We watch her take the Tupperware to the car. She has mittens on and she is singing—no words, just a light hum. This is usual for Charlene. She almost always hums and doesn't sing with words.

We watch her lock the house, get in her car, take the mittens off, crank the car and drive over. She is still singing. We don't hear her when the saw cuts in, but we see her mouth move.

She parks next to Mr. Dawson's twenty-year-old truck. "That's a long time with a good truck," is how Mr. Dawson puts it. He pats his truck hood a lot. The only rust on the truck is around the chrome.

"Can y'all help me?" Charlene asks, rolling down her window.

Tommy cuts off the saw. I put down my hammer and we walk out into the heat.

If you don't request biscuits, Charlene usually brings sandwiches—turkey or roast beef or a mixture of both with mayonnaise and white bread. But if you request biscuits, she brings meat, vegetables, iced tea, biscuits.

I carry the three vegetables in a Tupperware stack. Tommy has the meat and the iced tea. I wish I had the mittens—the vegetables are hot—but Charlene is wearing them as she reaches into the backseat for the biscuits and some cups and napkins and forks and plates. The cups and napkins and forks and plates clunk around in a cloth bag.

Tommy and I line up five 2x4s over two sawhorses. Mr. Dawson brings out the tablecloth he keeps in his office. We put all the food and accessories on top of the cloth. The cloth is covering the boards. The cloth is red and white checkered and covers the boards completely.

We weren't supposed to have a lunch break, but Charlene has brought a lot of food.

"Let's take a small break," Mr. Dawson says, sighing, and looks at his watch. Mr. Dawson is sweet to Charlene in this way. He likes to reward good work, so he smiles as he picks up a biscuit. He puts the biscuit to his mouth. It is steaming.

"Where are my chairs?" Mr. Dawson wants to know. He looks at me, then he looks at Tommy.

Tommy and I go to the corner where the pile of wooden blocks and sawdust are swept. We climb on top of the pile, grab the folding chairs, and bring them to the two sawhorses.

We all sit down. Charlene serves our plates. She hums while she serves us.

"Thank you," I say.

"Thank you, Ma'am," Tommy says.

Tommy and I have placed the chairs under the tin roof so we

will be out of the sun. It is hot today. The tin roof is popping like chicken necks. Big, loud chicken necks.

Jack is still in the field painting, and the chairs are facing the field so, while we eat, we watch him. It is the first time we have all watched Jack together.

"That boy sure does love to paint," Charlene says.

"Yes," Mr. Dawson agrees. His mouth is full of food. His words are all grumbly.

"You think he would paint our house?" Charlene asks.

"I don't think he does that kind of painting," Mr. Dawson says.

"He doesn't," Tommy agrees.

"Well, he could learn," Charlene says. She always likes to give jobs to people who don't have jobs.

There are a lot of people on Bucking Street who don't have jobs, and you can find them doing yard work at Charlene's house or painting her house or painting her fence that runs between Charlene's house and the Truss Company. They clean her house on the inside, too. They walk to the Truss Company late in the afternoons after they finish and Mr. Dawson pays them.

"I don't think you can teach him much," Mr. Dawson says about Jack. Mr. Dawson's mouth is full of food.

"I could teach him," Charlene assures us. "He sure is handsome. His back anyway," she adds. She's putting butter on a biscuit—using a knife—putting butter on the outside and on the inside of it. The biscuit is so hot, the butter melts all over, and drips on Charlene's dress, drips onto the floor.

"You want this?" she asks Tommy.

"No, Ma'am," he replies.

"You?" she asks me.

"No, I'm good," I reply.

We've both had enough biscuits.

It's the last one she's holding.

The butter keeps dripping. It's really yellow and making these blobby oil stains on her dress. A pretty blue dress. A big blue dress. There is a pocket on the skirt part. The pocket has a pattern of daises on it, and the daises look like waffles. For some reason, they look like waffles. There are blotched oil stains on the waffles on the dress now.

"Tommy. Gill. One of y'all take this biscuit to that boy. He needs to eat something," Charlene says.

I'm the closest to her, so I decide to take it.

"Yes Ma'am," I tell her. I walk out from under the tin into the sun. My eyes squint. I get a headache for a few seconds. Then it goes away. It is a brilliant day.

I walk out to Jack.

There is meat on my breath. I can smell the meat. Chicken. There are pieces of chicken meat in-between my teeth, and the biscuit is getting soggy in my hand.

The magenta is all gone from the painting. The painting is a real light red. This is what he's been painting with—light red. Tommy can tell me the color when I get back.

I'm concentrating on not tripping over the uneven dirt. It's a plowed field, and it sinks a little wherever I walk. Nothing was planted in this field, so the rows are bare. The field is gray looking—like clouds on a cloudy day. There are a few weeds.

I'm real close to Jack, close to his backside.

The blue shirt he's wearing is like the sky. He's sweating, too—under his arms, in lines down his back. He's sweating a lot.

He's not painting wild today, and he's not panting from all his sweating.

When he moves his brush, I see sweat drip from his black hair into the collar of his blue shirt—it's like the sky blue.

I keep my distance from Jack. I'm close to him, but I keep my distance not to disturb him.

This is the closest I've ever been to him. As I've said, I've seen him a lot from my truck when he was in the other field, but I haven't been this close before. I don't want to be a bother.

I watch him with the soggy biscuit. Watch him move his brush across the canvas left to right. Then right to left. North through south. He's not using the sponge, just the brush and lots of light red.

On the right hand side I see a face or a body—some type of figure. One arm, I think. A leg.

I move closer. The figure is a figure, I think, but more a ghost than real.

The biscuit is real soggy. My hand feels like a wet sponge, and I see he has painted a ghost figure on the right hand side of the canvas.

"That's a ghost," I say to him. I would have never been able to see this from the Truss Company.

Jack dips his brush in more white and red and carries a long stroke across.

Everything is quiet except for the sound of his brush brushing or sometimes some of his sweat hitting the water bottles or the plate of paint he is holding.

I feel weird about what I said about the ghost cause Jack won't answer me.

You shouldn't have said that, I tell myself. *You're disturbing him.*

"Hey," I say a little softer and more cautiously, "would you like a biscuit?" I'm whispering is what I'm doing.

Jack picks up a bottle, drinks some water, puts the bottle back down.

He picks up a tube of paint. The red.

He squirts the red paint onto the plate. He swirls the brush in the paint on the plate. He sweeps the brush across the canvas like a broom, like when I take the broom and sweep the Truss Company's concrete floor. Jack does this four or five times. He dips the brush in the paint again and again. Does it again like he's sweeping dirt off the canvas. Only it's red paint. He's not using white anymore.

The sun shines off the fresh layers and in some places, the paints bleed a little.

The biscuit is so soggy, I want to squeeze it, wring the butter and the sweat out. But then the biscuit wouldn't be good to eat. I've got to do something or the biscuit is going to fall apart.

Carefully, I walk closer to Jack.

I'm starting to sweat a lot.

I don't want to disturb him, so I go slow. Then I bend down, put the biscuit on top of a water bottle.

I look up as if I'm looking at the sun while I'm squatting down. I look at the side of Jack's face.

He has black eyebrows like his hair. Everything else—chin,

nose, cheeks, forehead—all of it is tan, not sunburnt. His skin is a deep brown tan like a shadow. Sweat is dropping from his chin. His face is wet like he's taken a shower.

The whole time I'm looking, he doesn't look at me once. Keeps painting. I can hear the brush going across the canvas. The brush makes the brushing noise.

I move off a few steps and start to walk away, but first, I take one more look at the ghost figure. The arm and leg are gone. The arm and leg have been swept off the canvas. The face has lines of red across it. The face doesn't look like a face anymore. Just a piece of one. The face is only half made.

Jack brushes more lines across.

I turn away and go back to the Truss Company.

*

"What did he say?" Charlene asks. "Will he paint my house?"

"He didn't say anything," I tell her.

"He's not eating my biscuit," she says and leans forward in her chair to get a better view of Jack and the biscuit of hers she sent sitting on the water bottle.

"He's probably deaf," Mr. Dawson says. "Most artists are, like Beethoven."

"We'll never get him to paint the house," Charlene is disgusted.

"He's not deaf," Tommy says. Tommy is finishing up his cup of sweet tea. "He's concentrating. That's all. Really concentrating."

"I want him to eat," Charlene says. "It's not healthy to not eat."

"He's got lots of energy," Mr. Dawson says.

"He needs to eat," says Charlene. She leans back.

"Well," Mr. Dawson says and stands up, "we've got to get back to work. We've got to leave for Snead by 4." He taps his watch with his finger.

"Thank you for lunch," I tell Charlene and go get my hammer, lower my head. I shouldn't have disturbed Jack.

"Thank you, Ma'am," Tommy says. He walks over to the saw.

"You're welcome," Charlene smiles, hums a little. She lets the notes slip out of her mouth happily. I hear the Tupperware lids snap down on the bowls.

Mr. Dawson is folding the tablecloth. He helps his wife carry everything to her car.

"Come home early," I hear her tell Mr. Dawson. "You never come home." She points a finger.

"As soon as we get back from Snead," he promises.

Tommy turns on the saw.

Charlene cranks up her car, drives home.

Mr. Dawson goes into his office, picks up the dialup and dials. The box fan cranks up a notch.

I look out at the field at Jack, and he's painting.

*

It is 1:00. We have three hours to finish the truss order.

"Hurry up," Mr. Dawson says. He doesn't come out of his

office or hang up the dialup to say it.

If we don't hurry, Mr. Dawson's going to have to go to Bucking Street, get some extra help. That's extra money he doesn't want to spend.

I look over at Tommy, and he's only got about ten more boards to saw. He puts a board in place. Brings the saw across, and the saw screams. Nine more boards.

I hammer fast. Some of the nails go flying through the air cause I don't hit the head right. One of the nails goes all the way to the roof and *pings* where it hits the tin. The tin has been popping since 11:30 from the heat. It is popping louder now and sounds as if someone is dropping huge pecans and hickory nuts.

"Hurry up," Mr. Dawson says again.

I hear a door close, but it's not Mr. Dawson's office door. It's the back door to his house. Charlene has come into the backyard in her two-piece bathing suit. She has a towel, lotion, and her telephone. She stops at a folding chair, which is sitting in front of a bird feeder. She puts the towel in the seat of the chair and turns the chair to her left. She sits down. And I know what she is watching today. She's watching Jack.

I've been so busy hammering, I haven't noticed that Jack is painting faster than this morning, faster than at lunch. The red is almost all gone. The red is being replaced with a deep green. I wonder if the ghost figure is still there. So I concentrate on the right hand side, which looks very green now.

"What color?" I ask Tommy. He's finished with the boards and is helping me nail.

Tommy squints. "Forest green," he says. He puts the box of

metal truss plates on top of the table, hammers those over the joints.

"Forest?"

"Yes," Tommy says.

"Hurry up!" Mr. Dawson says. He's still in his office.

Jack flings a glob of green paint on with his hand and smears it across the canvas. His hand is all green and so is the cuff of his blue shirt.

"He's making a forest," I tell Tommy.

Tommy nods in agreement.

Tommy and I lift the truss over to the press and run the truss through so that the metal plates will flatten out on both sides of the truss and the truss will be sturdy. We lift the truss off the sawhorses and carry the truss to the truck, load the truss with the others.

They all look the same. They don't change one bit—trusses. Sometimes their measurements are smaller than at other times, but, in general, trusses are triangles with the same design, same brace boards on the inside.

"They always look the same," I tell Tommy.

"We've got to hurry," he says.

We go back to the table, start nailing another truss.

Ping—another nail flies up to the tin roof.

Boom—the roof answers.

Swoosh—Jack throws on another blob of green. An even darker green than the forest green. Or maybe it's just a darker shade of forest—the darkest part.

I hear Mr. Dawson say he'll pick up groceries in Oneonta, which is on the way to Snead, and I hear Charlene say she also needs some flour.

While Mr. Dawson is talking, Charlene hums. Then she says, "I need more flour, too." This is how she puts it. Then she hums some more. *Hmhmhm*—it goes like that when I can hear her. Sometimes it's higher, a whinny, *Ah-hah-ah* is how it sounds when she's whinnying.

We take a truss through the press, put it on the truck. The number of trusses is starting to add up.

Faster and faster I'm hammering. Tommy's hammering.

Through the press. To the truck.

Hammering, hammering. Through the press. To the truck.

It's like a song, our own song, when we get into this kind of rhythm.

"Hammering, hammering. Through the press. To the truck," I sing in a low voice, stretching out the words *pressss* and *truckkkk* through my teeth. I'm trying to sing the same notes Charlene does when she says, *Hmhm, lalalaaaala, hmhmhmmmm.* And I laugh when I finish singing the same line in the same way as Charlene cause I'm being silly.

Tommy doesn't sing.

And when we move the trusses over from the table to the press, I look at Jack.

I can only see his jeaned legs because he's moved from the front of the canvas to the backside of the canvas. He still is using green. He's using both of his hands now. And he dashes on a blob from the left. Splashes on a streak from the right. Then he smears all of it in with his hands. He smears the top of the easel, the legs of the easel. And sometimes his head bobs to a corner, and I can see his face. We can all see it, if we want to.

"Hurry up!" Mr. Dawson shouts.

Jack's face is very tense. He does not, not once, look away from the painting, from all the green he is making.

Through the press to the truck we go.

Boom goes the tin.

"Hurry up!"

And Jack has painted the easel completely green. He's painted all but one of his water bottles. He walks around, squeezes out all of his tubes of paint—orange, red, yellow, blue—everything, squeezes the colors into his palm, then turns his back to us again.

He lifts both his hands, throws blobs of paint at the sun as if he's throwing a ball for the sun to catch. He moves his hands like windshield wipers across the sky.

"He's painting the sky," I tell Tommy.

But the sky isn't changing color.

"That boy has got a lot of energy," I hear Charlene say into her phone. "He has to be hungry."

I see some paint blob off of Jack's hands and fall to the ground, but I can also see where the paint should go—where the orange would've smeared and the red, the yellow, if the colors had stuck to the sky. I can see this, see the different patches of color while he paints and we put the last truss on the truck.

It's 3:30.

"Damn good job. You did it, Gill. Tommy." Mr. Dawson is happy. He runs his fingers across each truss and counts the number out loud.

Jack must be tired because he's stopped painting the sky. He is sitting on the ground looking at what he's just done.

It is his best work, I think. Even if the sky didn't hold it, even if you can't see it.

"28, 29, 30," Mr. Dawson says. He turns to us. "We're going to get to Snead early!" Mr. Dawson slaps me on my back. Slaps Tommy.

"Let me call Charlene. Tell her we're leaving," he says and trots back to his office. Mr. Dawson is wearing slacks. As he trots, his slacks rub, a sound like wind blowing through a forest of trees.

Mr. Dawson closes his office door.

Tommy and I get some water.

"He's worn out," I say to Tommy and point to Jack with my cup.

Tommy nods. "Yes," he says. Both Tommy and I are breathing hard. Our T-shirts are soaked with sweat.

"Are you okay?" Charlene has gone over to the fence that separates her backyard from the Truss cCompany and the field. The fence is white. Somebody from Bucking Street painted the fence three weeks ago. Charlene is talking to Jack.

"Are you okay?"

Jack doesn't answer her. Doesn't talk to her.

"I love you, too," she says into the phone.

She lingers a while longer at the fence. She is singing "la la lo." She sings the notes real soft, real slow—*La . . . la . . . lo . . . . . .* is how it sounds, like a bird.

Charlene is red, lobster red, between the top half and bottom half of her bathing suit. The bathing suit has a toaster and toast popping out of toasters print on top and bottom. I thought they were polka dots or seashells, but from here they look like toasters. The toasters are silver. The toasts are white and brown. The bathing suit is blue like her blue dress.

Charlene's hair is wet with sweat on the ends. It turns her hair curlier than ever.

"Bye now," she calls to Jack and waves. He doesn't answer. She turns and goes inside. She sings "lo . . . . . ." just that one note all the way in.

"Let's go," Mr. Dawson says. We get in the company truck.

*

It's late Wednesday night, early Thursday morning, 2:30 a.m. And I've got this feeling Jack has not gone home. I'm also hungry, so I leave my house, get in my truck and drive to the American Truss Company.

Lights are off at Mr. Dawson's house. He was so happy today that we saved him money, he took us out to eat at the Golden Corral in Snead. I had a ribeye, fully loaded potato and a salad with blue cheese dressing. There is nothing better than blue cheese.

Lights are off at the Truss Company, too, and I park my truck so my lights shine through the tin shelter out into the field. I spot the green easel and canvas and painted water bottles and even the white glow of the biscuit offered to Jack at lunch.

Sitting on the ground, the same as when we left for Snead, is Jack.

I cut the lights off and step out of the truck.

Waffle House, I remind myself. I've decided to go to the Waffle House instead of the Huddle House when I leave here. That steak made me hungry.

I go to the end of the Truss Company and stop. I don't want to disturb Jack like I did during lunch. I put my hand against the pile of wood chunks and sawdust, and I watch him.

I can't see where he painted the sky anymore. I know the painting is there, but it is too dark.

But Jack isn't looking at his painting. He is looking up at the stars. There are many tonight. No moon, so the stars shine clearer, form a dome to the trees. The trees come down the ridge and surround the field.

I know what he wants. Jack wants to paint those stars. As I look at them, I think about what colors Jack would paint them, and I am no longer hungry.

*

"I'm happy."

It's officially Thursday now and those are the first words Mr. Dawson greets Tommy and me with.

Jack is in front of his canvas, painting over the green with a yellow.

"Primrose yellow," Tommy says.

"Primrose," I second. The sound of it is very pretty.

Jack's hands are caked in colors and dirt. His shirt is a light purple.

"Lavender," Tommy says.

Charlene is leaning across the fence. She is leaning across the fence further into Mr. Pardee's field than she did yesterday.

She has her rose dress on. It is a pink dress with red roses all over the fabric. There is a bow at her waist, a sash. Every now and then she waves at Jack, but he never looks at her. Today, she is singing words.

"Baby so sweet, so sweet, my baby, you are," she says. She sings louder than she did yesterday, but she doesn't sing as often. Only when she waves at Jack.

"That boy really does love to paint," Mr. Dawson says. "I'm going to ask him to paint my house."

Tommy and I stand by the worktable as Mr. Dawson walks out to the field to talk with Jack.

Charlene waves. "Where is my baby?" sings Charlene.

Mr. Dawson smiles and waves to Charlene. Jack keeps painting.

Pretty soon, Mr. Dawson is walking to the truss company shelter. He's not smiling.

"He's deaf," Mr. Dawson says. "Deaf like Beethoven," shaking his head. "He won't look at me." Mr. Dawson rubs his chin.

"Concentrating," Tommy urges. Tommy painted when we were in high school. One of the few who did.

"Well, there's nothing to do today." Mr. Dawson looks at Tommy. He looks at me.

"Let's clean up," he says and goes into his office.

Tommy and I start to clean up.

It is a slow morning and I can see this in the way Jack paints. He sweeps long sweeps across the canvas as if his brush, his hand is a wave of the ocean—a calm wave.

Tommy and I spend most of the morning moving the pile of

wooden blocks in the corner of the Truss Company shed to the big pile of leftover boards behind the shed in the field. We keep back any pieces we might need later on.

The pile in the back is getting pretty big, and we'll have to start a fire soon.

Tommy walks around picking up all the nails I pinged to the roof yesterday, and I take a broom, sweep the sawdust. I make my sweeps like Jack makes his—long, slow. The broom makes a brushing sound, and I think about the ocean.

At 11:30 Mr. Dawson comes out of his office. I don't hear Charlene, and I don't see Charlene on the fence line. She must be inside cooking. I smell biscuits.

"I'm going to Oneonta to get us some food," Mr. Dawson says. This makes the second lunch in two days he has treated us to. And there was the supper at the Golden Corral.

"How does chicken sound?" Mr. Dawson asks. "And cole slaw? And biscuits?"

But I smell biscuits already baking next door. I look at Tommy. I can tell he smells them, too.

"How does that sound?" Mr. Dawson says again.

"Isn't Charlene baking biscuits?" I ask.

"No," he says. "She didn't want to bake today."

"Chicken sounds good to me," Tommy says.

Mr. Dawson looks at me. I look at Mr. Dawson.

"Mr. Dawson—" I start, then stop.

Neither one of us say a thing.

"Mr. Dawson—" I stop again. "Don't go," I tell him.

"What?"

“Don’t go, Mr. Dawson.” I put my hand on his shoulder.

I look at Mr. Dawson. Mr. Dawson looks at me.

“It’s a free meal.”

“I know,” I tell him. “But you need to go home and eat.”

Mr. Dawson moves back a step so my hand is no longer resting on his shoulder. He rubs the sweat from his head. Being out here, out of his office with me and not in front of his box fan is making him extra sweaty.

“I’m going to get chicken,” he says. “And unless you tell me right now, ‘I don’t want any chicken,’ I’m getting you some chicken, too, Gill.”

I put my hand out again, but he quickly turns and heads to his truck. His slacks are rubbing fast against his legs.

“Why don’t you stay here?” I call after him.

“I’m getting chicken,” he says and slams his truck door.

Soon he’s on the highway.

*

The smell of biscuits baking in hot, dry air is a powerful thing. It makes you hungry that very minute, that very second.

Charlene still has on her pink, red rose dress with the sash as she walks out to her car with a plate in her hand. The plate is stacked perfect with biscuits.

“Baby . . . ba-by . . . ,” she sings, but she is singing softly, quietly now.

She pulls her mittens off. Cranks up her car.

While she’s driving over, Tommy asks, “Do you think she’ll

let us have a biscuit?"

I shake my head, no, and look out at Jack.

Jack is still slowly drifting his brush across the canvas, moving the brush as if it is the ocean. The yellow is really bright now, bright as the sun. It isn't a banana yellow. The easel is still green.

Charlene parks her car and steps out. She smooths her dress. Then she reaches into the back seat for the plate.

"Hello, Gill. Tommy," she says politely. She is wearing perfume and makeup. Her face is powdered. She is not sweating. The perfume is strong, but the biscuits carry the strongest smell.

"Those are nice biscuits," Tommy says. These biscuits are bigger, fluffier than what she brought yesterday.

"Thank you," says Charlene.

She doesn't stop while she talks, doesn't offer us a one. She is humming very, very softly now. I can barely hear her.

She passes by us under the popping tin and out into the hot sun, the field. *Boom* the tin shouts while she walks to Jack.

"Hmmmmmmmm," Charlene softly answers.

I almost follow after her.

Tommy pulls out two chairs, turns them to the field. He sits down.

I move to the edge of the Truss Company shelter, to where the woodpile was. I watch Charlene approach Jack.

"Hello, Boy. Jack," she says sweetly. She picks up a biscuit. I can still see the steam from the butter smoking off the top. "Would you like one of these. I know you must be hungry." She has the plate full of biscuits in one hand and the single biscuit in the other.

Jack dips his brush into a blob of black—whips the color onto the canvas.

"I know you must be hungry," Charlene repeats, moves the biscuit in front of Jack's nose.

He dips into the black and whirls it across the canvas, making loops from left to right.

Charlene pushes the biscuit to Jack's mouth.

"Open up," she says.

Jack won't open his mouth.

"Take a bite," she says.

Jack loops more loops on the canvas.

"I made these for you," Charlene says sweetly, and she steps closer to him. She is closer to him than I was yesterday.

"Take a bite," she says and puts her mouth up to his ear. She's humming, but then her humming stops.

She's whispering something or kissing him or licking him. I can't tell. But I'm pacing back and forth from one side of the Truss Company shed to the other in front of Tommy who is sitting in the chair on the left.

Boomboomboom goes the roof.

Licklicklick goes Charlene.

And Jack makes bigger and faster swirls.

And Charlene won't remove her mouth from Jack's ear, but she needs to move her mouth off Jack's ear.

Boom.

"You're disturbing him," I shout while I'm pacing. Neither one of them moves.

Boom boom.

"You're disturbing him."

I head out into the field, almost tripping over the uneven ground.

"Ma'am."

They don't budge.

I stop a few feet away. All the black swirls have formed a fence—a chain link fence. And on the right hand side he has left it yellow, a yellow where the black fence isn't.

"Leave him alone," I tell her. I don't say it loud. I say the words very calmly. "Ma'am, leave him alone, please." I am sure I am saying the words calmly.

Charlene removes her mouth from Jack's ear.

I look at Charlene. Her hair is in tight curls. She has on earrings.

"You're disturbing him," I say. "Ma'am," I say, "he's painting."

She glares at me. Her face is still sunburnt from yesterday.

"He's disturbed," she says. "He won't talk to me. He won't do anything."

Jack keeps painting. His ear is wet, and the sun makes his ear glimmer.

"Who's going to paint my house?" she wants to know. She's standing next to Jack. I'm afraid she's going to hit him with the plate of biscuits.

"You better say something," she says to Jack.

"I'll paint it," I tell her.

And she and I look at each other, the only sound being the brush going across the canvas.

Charlene isn't happy, but she puts the biscuit back on the plate with the other biscuits and walks past me to the shelter. She still isn't sweating.

I hear her car crank. I don't turn and watch her leave.

I hear the engine cut off. The door to her house opens and slams shut. I don't hear Charlene singing.

I stand a few feet away and watch Jack paint. I don't make a noise.

It's not really a fence—it's night. He keeps adding more and more black until the yellows are only dots, are only stars, and on the right hand side is this one real bright yellow like the sun coming up or the moon.

"I've got you some chicken," Mr. Dawson calls out from behind me, so I turn away and head back to the Truss Company.

Mr. Dawson has the tablecloth spread out, and Tommy is still in his chair already eating a second piece.

I pick up my chicken and take a bite, then spit it out. I'm not hungry.

"What's wrong?" asks Mr. Dawson.

"Not hungry," I tell him.

After lunch, we clean around the outside of the shed. Mr. Dawson is in his office on the dialup. I don't see Charlene. She's somewhere in the house. She's still not singing.

"Charlene says you're going to paint the house, Gill," Mr. Dawson reminds me as we turn off the lights.

I nod that that is true.

The fan blades chip at the front metal screen of the box, then stop. It's 5:00.

"You can probably get most of the painting done this weekend."

I nod that this is also true.

"I'll get some paint and brushes tomorrow," he says. He smiles. Mr. Dawson is happy.

I nod again.

*

Tonight is Thursday night. It is early Friday morning. It is 2:30. I leave my house and drive out to the Truss Company. All of the lights are off at Mr. Dawson's house.

I see Jack through the headlights and turn them off.

He isn't sitting down. He is at the canvas.

I get out and walk to where he is.

He is still painting the stars and night. He keeps going over the black with more black and dotting the yellow with more yellow.

"Primrose," I say quietly. The word is very pretty.

This night is just like last night. There are many stars. There is no moon.

On the right hand side of the painting is a big yellow space where the moon is supposed to be, but it's not.

I look up at the stars. Then I look down.

On top of one of the water bottles is the biscuit I brought Jack. I know that it isn't soggy anymore. The sun has dried it out.

I walk closer to Jack and keep looking at the biscuit until finally I pick the biscuit up. But I'm not hungry. And at first I think I should give it to Jack because he really does need to eat.

I watch Jack dip his brush in more black, then more yellow.

I move over to the paint, smell it, the oil.

The blobs are wet so I can see the light of the stars reflecting in the fresh layers of paint. The yellow kind of glows.

And I think of something, think I know what Jack needs to do with his painting.

I lift the biscuit, then dip it in black, swirl the biscuit for several seconds in the black on the plate, then I stretch my hand to the right hand side, the yellow spot, and brush the biscuit across the yellow.

Jack does not even look at what I'm doing. Does not turn at all. What he does is move. He moves over a step so I can stand next to him, so I can be close to the canvas.

I dip the biscuit into the black again and paint on another wet stroke.

At first the lines look like a fence. But I know what I want to do. I add more and more layers until the black is thick with pieces of biscuit, thick with shine. I know what I have to make.

Hawk

—

My brother stopped the truck, and he pulled off the curve before we got to our house on County Road 15.

Above us a bird's black wings were sweeping sky from one side of the road to the other. It was a hawk. I loved to watch them, not only for their long wings, but for their gliding, the sweeping of the sky, which seemed so free to me. Somehow they knew what breath was and had invented it, riding the sky for so long. They knew how to stop and start the lungs. Watching made me aware my own lungs were in a rhythm of emptying, filling—that I was breathing, too.

"I can shoot it," my brother said.

"No way," I told him and smiled. No matter how good of a shot he was, he couldn't hit a flying bird—not that far up. Against the law to kill hawks anyway.

"Watch me." He took his rifle off the rear-window rack, booted open the door, pushed the barrel against the side of the window frame with his hand.

The hawk made long drawn out loops and sailed higher.

"No way you going to hit him," I told him. And the longer my brother stood there, motionless, the better I felt. No, he wasn't going to be able. He's not that good.

"I can do it in one try," he said, his head flat on the stock, one eye shut, one eye at the scope.

"You're full of it," I said. "I'll buy you a beer if you do."

"Alright," and he jumped in the bed of the truck, steadying the rifle on the roof of the cab.

I looked up at the hawk, diving a little, then bringing its wings out to slow and glide. I looked around the curve for the sheriff or game warden, but mostly I watched the hawk's kite-sweeping, its body and wings, until finally the hawk dove in, lit on a sweet gum branch. My brother shifted behind me.

I wanted to yell, *He's not flying. You can't do it unless he's flying.* I waited and waited, the shot never coming when I thought it would, but it did. The hawk fell from the sweet gum, a few limbs making room.

My brother got down from the bed of the truck, headed to the small woods.

"One beer," he called over his shoulder, and he didn't come out of the woods until the hawk's left wing was gripped in his hand like a fan. The head of the bird bobbled with my brother's walking.

He was saying something about why I shouldn't bet against him. I didn't hear. I was checking my own breathing unable to get still.

"You owe me," he said when he shut the cab door, the hawk slung on the truck bed, and my brother pulled down fast to the Mustang Stop before I could forget what I owed him and spend my money elsewhere. The wind blew sand and trash across the bed against the hawk's feathers.

STOP

—

She opened the passenger door, lifted a handful of pennies out of my console, whooped 'em up, clanging those pennies inside her fist, her hollering rising, rising, until pennies got flung and they sailed like copper rain sideways-popping the red metal sign.

"State Taxes on Pussy!" she yelled, busting my ear with that drum. Then she swung down level—"You got to drink to seal the deal"—and handed the hooch over. I'd never drunk out of a hooch until tonight, but each time I did I swear I tasted the inside skin of the animal it was cut from. Alcohol kills germs, I reassured myself, even if something four-legged and clomping was brought up with the taste.

She took a swallow deep. "Um," she said, her throat getting knocked hoarse. My tongue was burning. "Welcome to Alabama, Richard."

I hit the pedal and drove.

"Hey, you near where I want to take you," she said. "Turn."

I spun the wheel, and we swooped onto a dirt road that tunneled under branches that broke up the heavy-bottomed moon. At bald spots, the moon pieced itself back together. Faster, faster I drove the washboard road. My red taillights unable to wake the dust.

I stopped hard—had to—my grill was at the teeth of a barbed fence, and she just laughed. "You killing it tonight, Richard. Maybe you should lay off the hooch a while."

Pride said otherwise and I took another hit. "I'm good." But the buzz in the engine was in me.

Door got opened. She walked up to a post, tackled it with her shoulder, which caused the wire lip to flip off and the cattle gate to fall into a tangled mess she raked aside. I knew how to open gates from when I was a kid working my father's cows, moving their tail-whipped hides from one field to the next until my father's bad luck. A bull hoofed him in the heart, and cracked his center bone, stopped the beating in him for good. When I got old enough, I left for Atlanta, left my brother the farm.

Right now my brother and his family were on a condo island in Florida they'd rented out—my widowed mother, too. I told them I needed to stop for a quick bite before getting back on the road. But *she* was at the diner where I stopped. *She* slung her hooch in the booth seat opposite mine and asked, "You from Alabama?" Her skirt brushed across the orange leather. "No, you're not" was her own answer. I wondered what it was about my choice of meat—snapper—and three vegetables—salad, cabbage, and candied yams—that betrayed.

"I got a place," she said, pinning curls behind her ears with bobby pins so the red in her face and the broken nose that had fixed itself could be seen brighter, "I want to take you." This was an hour ago.

When we got up and out of the booth, I heard someone say to someone, "Hoochie's got her a man."

Now we were here.

"Come on in," Hoochie said with a curtsey.

I popped the gas and shot forward. She pulled the gate taut and popped the wire back over the corner post and got in. Before us was the wide as hell open, too bumpy a field for me to floor it. My car's low-n-tight, so I kept the gear in first.

"Your land?" I asked.

She said, "I know the owner. He hasn't gotten round to cutting, just look." Her hand flitted at the windshield. "A waste of hay but pretty."

The high grass was brown in the headlamps. Back in Atlanta the governor had prayed on the capitol steps for an end to our long drought. All his prayer got us was water restrictions.

"I hope there's cows here," I said.

"Stop," she said. I did.

As far as my lamps could throw light, the open pasture kept going wider and wider. Trees were knuckled over barbed wire somewhere, but, if I tricked my mind, I could believe they weren't. The grass swirled and rolled like the ocean where I was supposed to be instead of here, dipping a toe in water, breathing in salt, then drinking the salt away with glasses of icy lime tequila, trying to figure out what to say to my brother and his family I had not seen in years.

Hoochie reached across, turned off the ignition. "Come on, Richard," she said, "wake up," and we pushed our doors against the wind pushing back.

"See that moon? Beautiful." She pointed.

I do-si-doed around, got to her and grabbed her moony hip. "Beautiful," I said. We hadn't kissed yet and I wanted a whirl.

She jumped. "You got to take me slow."

"There things I want to do," I said.

"Don't worry, we'll get to those things, but do you know what I want?"

Which confused the hell out of me. I mean, I was getting picked up by a woman at a buffet in Alabama, and we were heading out to do some fucking—that was the *want*, right? I'd done this kind of thing before. Though I was the one making moves, not the other way around. And usually it was a honkytonk, not a diner. And always me and whoever she was wound up at a Fabulosoed motel, or we wrestled out of our clothes sweating in my car over the gears if we were drunk and out of money. I'd never been taken by anyone to a field.

"I'll let you in, I promise," she said with sugar like I was something she might lose if not sweetened up right. I've known that feeling before. Makes me a little sick. "Don't worry," she said. She put my hand back on her hip. I didn't realize I'd taken it off. Then she got to the ground and pulled me. The wet ground went through my jeans cold. She sighed. "Rained all day yesterday. A soaker. Lightning, too."

A lightning strike had just cut and run across my mind—she took it. Ever been around someone like that? They take what you're thinking before you can get it out of your mouth. They fish hook into your brain, I don't know. My guess is you let them in before realizing what's been done.

She got a hip on the earth proper, flipped over onto her butt. I tried to get on top, and had my hand on her skirt about to lift the seam, when she slammed me aside like a roped calf.

"I can't move as fast as you want, Richard." She lay back, crossed the hooch in her arms. She shut her eyes and breathed in.

"You could get hurt putting yourself in this kind of situation," I said. Hoochie didn't say a word to that, but we've all seen such stories on the murder night TV.

The grass swept up to down, catching on my hands and the cuffs of my jeans and my hair, and I wished I'd never stopped at that buffet. Should've eaten somewhere else alone, or never stopped to begin with. It was weird luck brought me here. Otherwise, I'd be nearer the Florida line, nearer a mother wanting the second son I'd once been, nearer an older brother so separate it was hard to believe we came from the same root. His family looked at me as if I come from another planet. I had given up farm life for 9-5 city work—crazy to do that. Despite the mistrust, there was the past where my father lived. I hoped once I got in their presence, his absence would be repaired—him chasing cows, cussing those cows into a pen, and cussing at me and my brother to give a hand. The good ole days. They were expecting me.

"Lying here like this," she said, "is much better when you got someone with. Even better when you don't know that someone. You haven't any idea what to expect from me, Richard. And that's freeing."

"You're reading my mind. I was just thinking about expectations."

"I'm just speaking my mind. Why you so worried?"

"Supposed to be on the road."

"But you chose me," she said.

"I guess I did." But why?

"Who knows," she said.

"Stop it," I said.

"What?"

"I can't have a thought you don't steal."

"I haven't taken a thing." She put the hooch aside, got up, stretched, and walked into the pasture. "We got a nice moon just for us," she called back. Her words kept carrying and swirling.

And it was, the moon had peaked out bright in the blue. She was at the bottom of the blue, pulling out the tails of her shirt, letting them flop. Then she pulled up her skirt and squatted. Piss hit the grass. Then she river-wiggled up.

"Hey, there," she said, surprised by something. She reached over, which made her backbone into a knotted rail. Once she straightened, she walked towards me giggly. Atop her was a sun bleached cow head with horns. She moved where the field couldn't get even, those legs of hers becoming the ones of the animal, clomping where hooves had kicked up grass and spun the black earth under the moon.

I felt like I was spinning. I turned sideways for a tree to grab hold of but there was none. I could run to the car, but my engine was crackling, cooling, too busy resting to be of help. Armies of ants and crickets hadn't shown up yet to nibble on me. They were busy burrowing into the ground, trying to get warm. I'd have to start digging to reach them.

"I don't know where I am," I said for this was craziness, the dangerous kind. I mean, she could try to kill me, impale me with a horn if she wanted.

Hoochie squatted, kissed my hand where I had raised it into a shaky *Please, no*. Then she took the cow head and laid it between my hips and gave me the lip of the hooch. She went down and took my ankle. Gently, she untied my shoe, tugged it off, and then the sock, and tickled the soft belly curve of my foot, which made her giggle more, which spread tiny shoots of cool to my toes.

"Come on now," she said when I didn't laugh. "Don't let your feelings get hurt out here. Come on, Richard, you with me."

"Who's me, Hoochie?" I whispered it for I did not know her real name.

She dropped my foot, pushed the cow's muzzle up to my chest and went for my ear. She blew the sound out of my funnel. My mind went blank. The wind stopped. By the time she had rolled over to undress in the grass, my skin had peeled off from ear to foot, felt that way, and I was left to shiver. The wind blustered, sailed up to the moon telling it about this spot where we were, and the moon whispered back, *I see, I see*, and the grass—still dry above the dirt despite yesterday's soaker—swept like fire, rolling atop itself cause it couldn't do anything but breathe.

James Braziel grew up in South Georgia on a small farm where he cut and hauled pulpwood and watermelons in the summers. That life, the people and land there were the first bones of This Ditch Walking Love, but it wasn't until he moved out to rural Alabama that the collection came to be. He now lives in a cabin he's building by hand with his wife, poet Tina Mozelle Braziel. He says that it is not an easy existence, but a worthwhile one. His days are spent hammering, sawing, cutting firewood, and writing when he's not teaching creative writing at the University of Alabama, Birmingham. He's the author of two novels: *Birmingham, 35 Miles* and *Snakeskin Road*—books about an environmental disaster in the South in the near future. His other work has appeared in journals and newspapers including an article he wrote for the *New York Times* about the tornadoes that struck Pratt City in 2011.*This Ditch Walking Love* took shape in the Murphees Valley section of the Cumberland Plateau in central Alabama. Where I live, ridges lift above ravines the creeks and small rivers have cut into being. And if you dig down in a field, the steel of a shovel or posthole digger will hit the chert in the soil, causing the ground to spark. That difficulty of breaking the land can be heard in the people here—we set flint to our words. Speaking this way is at the heart of *This Ditch Walking Love.*

PGIL2021USA